W9-BSZ-830

Chasing Jupiter

Other books by Rachel Coker

Interrupted

Chasing Jupiter

RACHEL COKER

ZONDERVAN®

ZONDERVAN.com/
AUTHORTRACKER
follow your favorite authors

ZONDERVAN

Chasing Jupiter
Copyright © 2012 by Rachel Coker

This title is also available as a Zondervan ebook.
Visit www.zondervan.com/ebooks.

Requests for information should be addressed to:
Zondervan, *Grand Rapids, Michigan* 49530

ISBN 978-0-310-73293-8

Cover design: Greg Jackson/Thinkpen
Interior design: Ben Fetterley and Sarah Molegraaf

Printed in the United States of America

12 13 14 15 16 17 /DCI/ 20 19 18 17 16 15 14 13 12 11 10 9 8 7 6 5 4 3 2 1

To Hannah and Ruth, my little sisters and best friends.
For always encouraging and supporting me,
and giving your opinions before I even had to ask for them.
I love you both!

Chapter 1

Every story has to start somewhere. Mine starts with a list written on a sheet of yellow construction paper, folded neatly into fourths, and pushed under my bedroom door so that I brushed it with my foot when I got up that morning. I had buttoned my blouse and was reaching for the doorknob when I felt the edge of the paper prick my toe. I bent down and picked it up. *Birthday List* was written in the corner in smudged pencil.

Cliff. I slipped the paper into the front pocket of my blue jeans. Then I bounded down the steps, two at a time, my bare feet pattering against the wood. My brother was already sitting at the kitchen table eating a bowl of Cap'n Crunch. I reached over to ruffle his hair, but he ducked at my touch and scowled. *Okay, so it's a nontouching day.* I pulled my hand back and dropped the list on the table.

"What's this?"

"Good morning, Scarlett." Cliff swallowed a mouthful of cereal. "It's my birthday list."

Yeah, I kind of figured out that much. I opened the refrigerator and searched for the carton of milk, but it wasn't inside. "Cliff, have you seen the …" I looked up and saw it sitting on the counter. *Oh.* "Never mind." The bottle of milk was warm under my fingertips. I frowned, twisted off the cap, and took a big whiff. *Sour.* Fighting back my gag reflex, I set the milk back on the counter and shut the refrigerator. "Who left the milk out overnight?"

Cliff continued to chew. I wondered if he'd had the good sense to eat his cereal dry. He folded his napkin into fourths and wiped his mouth. *Nah*. My guess was he'd rather use the spoiled milk than disturb his routine. I, meanwhile, would definitely be finding something else to eat.

I walked over to the bottom of the staircase and shouted, "Grandpop Barley!"

No answer, which meant he was likely still asleep. I sighed and headed back into the kitchen.

Cliff was finished with his breakfast by the time I came back in. He had laid his spoon out over his bowl and was staring at the placemat in silence.

"Um, Cliff, why don't you look in the pantry for a can of tuna fish? I have to get our lunches made and put in the paper bags."

"Okay." He shrugged and opened the pantry, pulling out a stack of cans. Then he proceeded to sit on the floor Indian-style and carefully line up the cans in front of him. Within seconds, they were arranged in order of largest to smallest, with all the labels facing forward. Cliff grinned and glanced up at me, motioning to his line of cans. I noticed his sandy hair stood straight up on his head, as if he'd ran a rake through it while it was still wet.

"Just a second." I grabbed two slices of bread and the jar of crunchy peanut butter out of the cabinet, looking longingly at the creamy jar just to the right. Grandpop Barley's smoother stash was strictly off limits to the rest of us, and you did not mess with his stash. As I slathered together my peanut-butter breakfast and laid out bread for the tuna fish sandwiches, I was even gladder there were only a few more days of school. Soon it would be summertime, with more time to bake and put together proper, home-cooked food. *I can get through this.*

Makeshift meal in hand, I grabbed the list off the table and squatted on the floor next to Cliff. "You want to tell me about this?"

He didn't look at me. "I already told you." One of the cans apparently wasn't quite straight enough for him, so he picked it up and carefully turned it until it was aligned with the rest. "It's my birthday list."

"Cliff, your birthday is tomorrow." I took a big bite of my peanut butter sandwich and leaned against the cabinets. The linoleum floor felt solid and cool beneath my faded jeans. "Even Santa Claus doesn't work on that short of notice."

He made a face. "I'm not asking for Santa Claus, Scarlett. This is June, not December. There's less of a need for gifts. It's all about supply and demand. It shouldn't be a problem."

"We'll see about that," I said dryly, placing the paper on the table. So he was all about lists lately. *Better lists than Spanish dictionaries, I guess.* I unfolded the paper and smoothed out the creases. "So let's go over this."

"My Birthday List," I read out loud. "By Cliff Blaine. June 6, 1969."

1. *One monkey from Japan*

2. *Two red bicycles*

3. *Three friends to play hopscotch with*

4. *Four licorice sticks*

5. *Five books on how to speak Spanish*

6. *Six pieces of chalk*

7. *Seven songs that I know all the words to*

8. *Eight moons in the sky instead of one*

9. *Nine boxes of macaroni and cheese*

10. *Ten green baseball hats*

11. *Eleven birthdays in one year*

12. *Twelve pancakes*

13. *Thirteen subjects to rule*

14. *Fourteen stuffed elephants*

15. *Fifteen Spanish battles*

When I finished, Cliff was staring at me with wide, unblinking eyes. I folded the paper and handed it back to him. "It's quite the list." I pressed my lips together, holding back a smile. "There are twelve days of Christmas. I guess birthdays have fifteen days?"

He shrugged. "Well, I figured I'd change things up."

I stood and started on the dishes while Cliff continued to play with the cans. I grabbed Mama's old apron off the hook behind the cabinet and flipped it inside out, wrapping it twice around my slim waist and tying it in a double knot. The soapy dishwater stung at the little cuts on my hands. *Ow.* I frowned at my dirty nails. It was a little before six in the morning, and the school bus would be coming in less than an hour and a half. *How do I have dirty nails already?* There was a nick above my pinky from last Tuesday when I jumped off my bike too quickly and fell on the gravel. I was just glad that Mama hadn't seen the dents on my handlebars. All she needed was one more example of my being a tomboy to set her over the edge. She was forgetting that it was 1969, not the 1940s.

I glanced over my shoulder to see Cliff still sitting cross-legged on the floor, staring at his cans. "Whoa! You got those cans really straight." There were eleven cans of different sizes lined up in front of the refrigerator. The largest soup cans were on the outside, followed by the vegetable cans, and then the little round tuna cans.

Cliff cupped his chin in his palm and stared at them, oblivious

"Battle of Belchite," I said.

"Fought in 1937," Cliff fired back.

"Seige of Gandesa."

"Easy—1938."

"Well, that's the last one." I laid *The Condensed History of the Spanish Civil War* on the table and strummed my fingers on the back cover. "Cliff, why do you need to know all these dates? What are you planning to do with all this information?"

He just shrugged and opened the book again, looking over all the photos of guerrillas, matadors, and guns.

I sighed and studied my fingernails. Now flour was mixed in with the dirt. *Great.* I pushed away from the table. "The bus will be here in about ten minutes, so we might as well go bring Grandpop Barley a piece of that pie."

We hiked up the back staircase to Grandpop Barley's bedroom. He slept in the what was basically the storage room upstairs, because the rest of us already had bedrooms by the time he came to live with us, and Juli refused to give up the one we both shared.

The door was shut. I nudged Cliff. "Open it," I whispered.

He shook his head slowly. "Grandpop was a great soldier in the Battle of Badajoz. He may cut off our heads with a machete."

I rolled my eyes. "What are you talking about? That was a Spanish battle, Cliff. Grandpop Barley is from North Carolina."

He shrugged and knocked on the door.

Silence. We stood fidgeting, our hearts thumping, until …

"Come in."

I pushed open the door and forced a large smile. "Hello, Grandpop Barley! We brought you some peach pie!"

Grandpop Barley was sitting in his faded blue armchair. A lopsided red tie hung around his neck, knotted tightly. He frowned when we entered the room, squinting from the light in the hallway. "What?"

"Peach pie." I held up the plate.

"Oh."

I walked forward, holding the pie out before me like a peace offering. "Would you like some milk to go with it?"

He smacked his lips and gave us a toothless smile. "What about some peanut butter?"

My stomach lurched. "On peach pie?"

Cliff stepped forward. "That is the most ridiculous thing I have ever heard."

Grandpop Barley's eyes darted toward Cliff, and he stood and started toward the door. "Get that pesky child out of my room," he grumbled. His gnarly fingers reached up to loosen the red tie.

I reached out and pulled his hands back down. "Cliff's just being Cliff. I'll get you some peanut butter." I dashed downstairs and rummaged around in the pantry. *Why on earth does one family need eleven cans of black beans? We only have six family members.*

I could hear Cliff shouting upstairs. *Oh, great.* I grabbed the peanut butter and made a beeline for the back staircase. "Cliff!"

My brother came bolting down the steps. "I cannot tolerate him!" He looked over his shoulder and glared at the open door. "That pesky Grandpop Barley!"

I rolled my eyes. "Just stay downstairs for now, okay?" I glanced at the clock above the front door. Almost eight ten. *Agh!* "Um, actually, go back upstairs and brush your hair, then go wait by the front door, okay? Don't let the bus leave without me." I shooed him down the stairs and ran back up to the attic, taking two steps at a time. I paused in the doorway, hesitant to enter. "Grandpop Barley?"

"Well? Did you bring the peanut butter?"

I stepped in the room. Grandpop Barley was sitting in his blue armchair again, his red tie slung over his shoulder. He was licking some peachy glaze off his finger and humming to himself. His eyes lit up when he saw the jar of peanut butter. I pulled out a spoonful and handed it to him. I could hear the bus honking outside. *Please don't leave without me, Cliff.* "Um, I really have to go. You're good, right? You don't need anything else?"

"No, no, this is just spiffy." His long pink tongue stretched out and licked the peanut butter off the spoon. He smiled. "Oh, I do love peanuts." He used his finger to shove the rest of the peanut butter onto the pie. "Yum."

Gross. I wrinkled my nose and left, shutting the door behind me. I could still hear him chuckling through the crack. Cliff was still standing at the front door, his arms folded across his chest and his brow lowered. Another loud honk, this one long and hard. I grimaced. Well, at least the school bus hadn't left yet.

Chapter 2

I have no idea how birthday dinners actually go in normal families, but I can guess. A fine home-cooked meal, presents, and a cake with candles and icing. But I couldn't remember the last time Mama cooked anything. Normally, I just fixed something for me and Cliff. And sometimes Grandpop Barley. And it wasn't that I was a bad cook or anything. I was actually really good. But really good doesn't exactly compare to Mom's home-fried chicken and rolls.

Needless to say, we didn't have anything close to a homemade meal for Cliff's tenth birthday. Mama worked late at the local plantation-turned-bed-and-breakfast and asked Dad if he could just take us all out in his truck, Old Clunker. So we drove twenty minutes to the nearest diner for burgers and fries. Everyone except for Grandpop Barley, who had insisted on staying home to eat some disgusting peanut-butter creation, and Juli, whom no one had seen since she came home from school that afternoon. But at least she had gone to school. With only three days until she graduated from high school, it didn't seem like classes were her focus at the moment.

Old-fashioned music drifted from the old jukebox in the restaurant corner from singers like Nat King Cole and Perry Como.

"I love this song." Mama took another bite of her cheeseburger then delicately brushed the crumbs off her face. "We bought this album when you were a baby, Scarlett. Juli used to like it. But I guess she doesn't listen to this kind of music anymore."

I shrugged. "Ziggy told her it was better not to 'feed at the trough of entertainment prepackaged for the masses.'" The waitress had given me a wiggly green straw for my soda. I took big slurps as the icy sweetness trickled down my throat. *Yum.*

Mama wrinkled her little white nose and shot a glance at Dad. "What kind of name is 'Ziggy'?"

"Um, I think it used to be 'Luke', but then he changed it." I licked the salt off my french fries and glanced around the restaurant. I couldn't remember Juli ever dating a guy with a normal name. Jimmy Twinkie might have been the worst. Plus Jimmy Twinkie had a beard, which was far from normal.

"Well, of all the ..."

Dad shook his head slowly, lifting a fry to his mouth. Mama looked ruffled, but she quieted down and stared at her fork.

Cliff arranged the french fries on his plate in a long line. "Hey, look, they resemble spears. Uno, dos, tres ..."

"How did you learn Spanish?" Dad's eyes focused on Cliff's bent head.

Cliff shrugged. "Scarlett reads *For Whom the Bell Tolls* to me."

Mama shot me a glance. "In *Spanish?*"

I forced a smile. "I checked out a Spanish dictionary from the library last year and learned a few words. But I was just sort of ad-libbing, really. Cliff likes it when the soldiers sporadically burst into Spanish. He says it makes it more realistic."

"Although, realistically, the soldiers would speak in all Spanish. But Scarlett only knows twelve words," Cliff added.

I nodded. The conversation was starting to feel stiff. I knew they didn't really mind what I did with Cliff as long as I watched him after school and made sure he didn't get into any trouble. But still. I thought the Spanish thing was cute. True, it was a little weird, but that was just Cliff being Cliff. They made me feel like I was being irresponsible by nurturing his strange habits.

I picked up my burger and smiled. "This is a really good burger."

Mama glanced at Dad and groaned softly.

● ● ●

Juli still wasn't home when we got back at half past seven. So I took Cliff up to Grandpop Barley's bedroom so we could watch the television. They were replaying footage of the astronauts' orbit of the moon from back on Christmas Eve. Cliff had bugged me all week to watch it again.

"Hey, Scarlett?"

I pulled the blankets up closer to my chin and snuggled into position on the floor. "Yeah?"

Cliff sat on the floor at my feet, frowning in concentration. "What type of material do you think their spacesuits are made out of?"

"Um, I don't know."

"Do you think that you could make me a spacesuit out of that material?"

I glanced at him. "I doubt it, Cliff. That would probably be really, really expensive. You know, if it's temperature-proof and everything."

"Oh." He looked back at the floor for a few moments. "Scarlett?"

"Yes?"

"Do you think ..." Cliff pursed his lips. "Do you think they might have a book about how spacesuits are made at the library?"

"No, I don't think they have that kind of book just yet."

"Well, do you think someone might be writing it now?"

I shrugged. "Maybe."

"Shush up. I'm tryin' to listen." Grandpop Barley shot me a glare from his spot in the old armchair.

I frowned and looked back at the television. The tiny attic room felt very cramped with the three of us squished together. *Why can't we keep the television in the living room where we can all get to it?*

"Look," Cliff breathed, his eyes glued to the screen. "There it is."

The Apollo 8 spacecraft was drifting through the blackness of space. Before them, the tip of the moon peaked on the screen, a pale gray on our black-and-white television. It shimmered and swayed just a little bit—otherworldly in its pale beauty.

"In the beginning, God created the heaven and the earth," a voice was saying, "and the earth was without form and void."

We sat entranced, listening to the words being read. Little tingles ran up my arms at what I was seeing. The moon. Outer space. On my television set.

They're actually out there. Outside of the earth, looking down on us like God or something. Shivers ran up my arm. *It just doesn't seem possible.*

And then I remembered that it wasn't live. That it had happened five months ago. Still, it felt weird to watch.

"And from the crew of Apollo 8, we close with good night, good luck, a Merry Christmas, and God bless all of you—all of you on the Good Earth."

The television cut to a commercial, the loud noise immediately drowning out the sacred moment.

"I want to ride in a rocket," Cliff whispered. He turned to me, his eyes large. "Has anyone ever taken a rocket to Jupiter?"

I shook my head.

"Well, I'm going to be the first." His shoulders straightened as his chest puffed out. "Captain Cliff Blaine—first astronaut on Jupiter." His little freckled face erupted in a dimpling grin before he sped out of the room.

I leaned back against the armchair and looked up at Grandpop

Barley. He was scowling at the television, his red tie tightly fastened around the collar of his blue cotton pajamas.

"What do you think? Would you like to ride in a rocket?" I grinned, hoping to coax a smile out of him.

He shook his head, wrapping his arms around himself. "Looks dangerous."

I rolled my eyes and turned back around, grabbing a book off the bed.

Two minutes later, Cliff burst back into the room, gripping a piece of yellow construction paper. He knelt on the floor and shoved it into my face. "What's this?"

"My birthday list. Remember?"

I rolled my eyes. "What, did you make some last-minute adjustments or something?"

"Just look."

He really was too much. But I unfolded the paper and looked back over the list. Everything was the same, except for now, scribbled in pencil at the bottom, it read:

16. Sixteen rockets to Jupiter.

I glanced over the paper at Cliff's face. "So now you're going to be an astronaut?"

He nodded. "I'll teach the aliens on Jupiter how to speak Spanish. And collect moon— I mean, *Jupiter* rocks."

I opened my mouth to say something when the door downstairs suddenly burst open and voices filled the hallway. "I don't believe you! How could you do this to me—to us?"

"Relax. It's not like it's permanent."

My ears pricked. Juli.

So she's home. A stone sunk to the bottom of my stomach. *What has she done now?*

Mama's voice was growing louder. "It's awful! It's beyond awful! How do you expect me to look at you?"

"I'd like to think you don't care how I look." Juli's voice was laced with hard sarcasm.

"Don't care?"

Cliff scrambled to his feet and ran to the staircase, leaning over the balcony. He squinted his eyes and then his mouth dropped into a small *O.*

"What is it?" I hissed.

He looked at me and shook his head. "Juli's hair is blue."

In a heartbeat, I was on the steps beside him, watching the scene below unravel. Mama was standing by the door, hands on her hips. Dad stood beside her, looking helpless and at a loss for words. And Juli leaned nonchalantly against the stairwell.

Her once beautiful, chestnut-brown hair was dyed a hideous pale blue. Hints of brown remained, zig-zagging down her back in thin, ugly streaks. She was wearing her boyfriend's old leather jacket, which she'd embroidered with pink and yellow flowers. Peeking out below the jacket was a floor-length purple dress and battered leather boots. I scrunched my nose. *What happened to my lovely, had-it-all-together sister?*

"Why did you do it?" Mama asked, throwing up her hands. "Did you want attention? From us? From your boyfriend? What's his name again?"

"Ziggy," Juli muttered.

"Ziggy! That's it! What kind of a person calls himself 'Ziggy'?"

Juli bristled. "What do you mean 'kind of a person'? Ziggy is just as much a person as anyone in this house! More so because he thinks for himself and makes his own decisions instead of relying on others to get by." The words practically spit out of her mouth.

Dad stepped forward. "Watch it, Juli. This is still my house, and these are still my rules." His face softened. "Your mother and I are just worried about you. We hear all kinds of things about foreign substances and alcohol and we just don't want—"

She shot him a dirty look before bounding up the stairs. "I'm eighteen! I can take care of myself!" She brushed by me and Cliff, glaring at us. "Creeps," she muttered.

Dad bounded up the steps after her, but she beat him to her bedroom and slammed the door shut. He knocked, but she didn't answer. Still angry, he stormed to the stairs and gripped the railing. The wood pulled beneath his hands, swaying a little. He stopped on the second step and stared at the rail. "Remind me to fix that," he muttered, before heading back down and into the kitchen.

Cliff glanced at me, but I motioned for him to keep quiet. Mama looked up and seemed to notice the two of us for the first time. "You two go to bed," she said, turning away. "Now." Her voice sounded strained and tight.

I nodded for Cliff to go and watched as he walked down the hall to his room, pausing to look over his shoulder before heading inside and shutting the door. I tried to open my door, but the knob was locked. "Juli!" I shouted, banging on the door.

"Go away!"

Junky-sounding rock music blasted through the door, making the walls vibrate. I sighed and positioned myself on the floor beside the door. *Maybe she'll get tired eventually and let me in.*

I tried to close my eyes and drift to sleep, but the guitar riffs rattled my brains. I groaned, wanting Juli to either shut it off and let me in, or turn up the music louder so I couldn't hear Mama crying in the kitchen.

Across the hall, Cliff's door opened and he poked his head out. Seeing me sitting on the floor, he ventured into the hallway and settled on the ground next to me.

"You're supposed to be in bed."

He wrinkled his nose. "I couldn't sleep with all the noise. So I made a new list." He handed it to me.

I sighed and unfolded it, smoothing out the wrinkles so I could read his messy handwriting.

Birthday List

1. *One happy family*

2. *Two good sisters*

3. *Three kisses for Mama*

4. *Four boys who are good to Juli*

5. *Five new records that don't sound scary*

6. *Six cookbooks for my sister Scarlett*

7. *Seven new ties for Grandpop Barley, even though he probably won't wear them*

I refolded the note and handed it back to Cliff, overwhelmed with a sudden urge to kiss him. I ruffled his hair instead, even though I knew he hated it. "I loved it," I whispered. "I hope you get everything on this list."

He nestled next to me in the hallway, and we listened to Juli's music for a while. My eyelids began to feel heavy, and my head started to swim, even with the beats coming from behind the door. Mama's cries were soft now, and I could hear Dad's comforting voice talking to her.

"Hey, knock, knock," Cliff said. His voice sounded loud in the quiet hallway.

"Who's there?"

"Luke."

I frowned. Cliff was pretty good at telling knock-knock jokes, but I hadn't heard this one yet. "Luke who?"

"Luke through the hole and you'll find out." He gave me his signature punch-line smile.

I leaned my head against the wall and closed my eyes. "That was a good one. I liked that one."

"Scarlett?" Cliff whispered.

I grunted.

"Can I still have a rocket to Jupiter, though?"

A smile tugged at my lips. I peeked at him through one eye. "Yes, Cliff. I will get you a rocket to Jupiter if it is the last thing I ever do. Promise."

● ● ●

The hot air offered little breeze, making my hair stick to the back of my neck. *Drat Mama for making me wear this dress to church when it's over eighty degrees outside!* I made a face. *And it's barely June.*

I was tired of wearing too-short dresses because of that stupid growth spurt I'd had last September, when my legs suddenly shot out from under me, not only catching me up to all the other sixteen-year-olds in Georgia, but also leaving me taller than most of them. Those long legs made keeping up with Mama's fast pace pretty easy. But Cliff lagged behind, huffing and puffing as he struggled to catch up.

I glanced over my shoulder at him and exhaled. "Mama, I'm going to walk behind with Cliff. We'll make it there just a few minutes after you. I promise we'll get there on time."

"Okay, but don't linger." Mama shot us a glance before hurrying ahead with Dad and Juli. "I don't know what they'll say when they see that girl's hair," she muttered.

I slowed my steps until I fell into step with Cliff. "Hello!"

He glared at me and looked at the ground, counting his steps. "Uno, dos, tres ..."

"Oh, so you're going to be difficult today? Okay, then. I'll talk to myself." My eyes wandered around aimlessly as we walked. "Isn't it a beautiful morning? A little warm, perhaps. Yes, a little warm, but it's a *dry* heat. At least it's not raining. But if it was raining, wouldn't that mean it was cooler out? Perhaps, but—" I stopped mid-sentence, my eyes locking with the eyes of another.

Frank Leggett, the son of the peach farmer. His light brown hair fell across his forehead, almost shiny in the morning sun. He carried a ragged notebook tucked under one elbow. And he was staring at me like I'd grown two heads.

I jolted to a stop in the middle of the street, unsure what to do. *Should I say something? Did he notice me talking to myself? Of course he noticed, or else he wouldn't be staring.* "Um, good morning," I said weakly.

Frank's brows rose. His eyes trailed over me toward Cliff, who was grumpily walking in circles and then back to me. "Why are you talking to yourself?"

Funny story … My mind raced, but I couldn't think of a logical reason. I sighed. *Let him think I'm crazy.* "I'm more pleasant company than any other person I can think of. No one else is as eager to listen to me as I am."

He stared at me blankly for a moment. Then a smile broke on his face, slowly at first but then blossoming into a full-out grin. He had a wonderfully handsome face when he smiled, like the difference between a small flame and a blazing fire. His eyes were a gold-green, crinkling up at the corners. For three and a half glorious seconds, I was at a loss for words.

Then, as quickly as the smile came, it left and he was Frank Leggett again. Frank Leggett, the socially inept. Frank Leggett, the good-looking boy who was too moody for any of the girls to want to go steady with. Frank Leggett, the son of the peach farmer.

He nodded and turned, heading toward the church. I followed

behind, dragging along Cliff and wanting to kick myself. *Stupid, stupid.*

Pastor Greene's voice boomed through the church walls. "Good morning! And isn't it a wonderful morning to be in the Lord's house?"

My eyes squeezed shut. *Oh, great.* Frank pushed open the church door, and I braced myself. Sure enough, everyone turned around to watch the three of us slip in the back. Frank seemed unfazed and headed toward his family's pew.

Mama frowned at me. Beside her, Juli was holding back a smile, her hair even more hideously blue in the morning light. She looked frightful. Gorgeous, but frightful all the same. Our family would surely be the talk of Georgia that afternoon.

I lowered my eyes and led Cliff to where our family sat. I settled in my seat directly behind Dotty Greene, the pastor's wife. Her blonde hair was piled up in a beehive and obstructed my view.

"Please stand to sing," Pastor Greene said, pulling out a hymnal.

I flipped through pages in the hymnal until we came to the right hymn. *How Great Thou Art.* I wrinkled my nose. *Why do they all have 'thee's and 'thy's? Why not 'y'all'?*

I didn't really care that much about church or about the music or the sermon. I never gave much thought to God or heaven. I mean, the way I saw it, I was only sixteen. I had a long time before I really had to worry about getting "right with the good Lord," and all that. But what I did find intriguing was the pastor's wife's singing voice.

The music swelled to the chorus, and Dotty Greene's voice began to raise and waver. "Then sings my soul!" she belted out in a high, screechy voice. And then suddenly it dropped, breaking over a low note.

My eyebrow shot up. Because no matter how bad it sounded, it sure was interesting. *At least she sings with enthusiasm.* I tucked away a grin from the side of my mouth. *A whole lotta enthusiasm.*

Chapter 3

The last few days of school passed by in a blur. It had been a hot spring and an early summer. By mid-June, the peach trees were loaded with fruit and Georgia smelled sweet and sticky again. We were free to roam from dawn 'til dusk.

That was the summer of 1969, and I was sixteen years old. Thanks to Mama's prodding, I'd finally let my hair grow out, and it was the first summer I could run around with my loose waves whipping around me in the wind. It made me feel free and a little bit wild.

On our first official day off of school, we didn't have anything better to do than lie around, watch the clouds, and talk about nothing.

Cliff loved running his fingers though my ponytail. We'd sprawl out by the fence in the backyard and stay like that for hours, his hand tangled in my long auburn hair. That's what we were doing on a Monday. Just lying there and breathing in and out in silence.

Cliff took a deep breath and let it out, his chin tilted up at the sky. "Say, Scarlett?"

"Yeah?" My eyes were closed, and the sun felt so warm and soothing on my face.

"When are we going to build a rocket to Jupiter?"

A frown pinched my forehead. *Oh, I forgot I promised him that.* Obviously Cliff wouldn't have forgotten. I'd never known him to forget anything.

I closed my eyes. "Sometime, I guess."

Cliff sat up abruptly, frowning at me. "No! Every time you say that it means you're never going to do it! Scarlett never keeps her promises to Cliff!"

My eyes flew open. *Whoa, referring to himself in third person— not good.* I pried his fingers out of my hair. He was making it even more of a snarled mess. "Well, I promised you I would, didn't I? And I *always* keep my promises."

He settled back down, pacified by my response. I did always keep my promises, unlike most people. A promise spoken by Scarlett Blaine was a promise kept.

I rested my head on my forearms and stared up at the sky. Little wisps of clouds floated by like ships drifting across the deep blue sea. The grass was warm and soft under my skin. "So is that what we're going to do this summer? Build a rocket?" I asked.

"To Jupiter."

"Right." I glanced at him out of the corner of my eye. His chin was tilted back up toward the sky. I wondered if his thoughts were always up in the clouds, hovering above those of the rest of us. "What are we going to build it out of? Wood?"

"I don't think we'd ever make it to space in a wooden rocket ship. It would burn up from the sun!" He frowned. "No, we'd have to cover it in some kind of metal. Metal sheets, maybe, like the kind they used to cover the warehouse last fall."

Metal sheets. I ran up the calculations in my head. "Cliff, that'll cost a lot of money. How are we going to get it? I don't have a job."

He bit his lip, thinking hard. "We could do a tap show act."

"Neither of us knows how to tap dance."

"Oh." Cliff fell silent for a moment. "Well, you're pretty good at baking pies. You'll sell pies, and we'll use the money to buy wood."

"Sell pies?" I tried to imagine myself standing at a pie stand, selling pies on the street. "No one would come."

"Yes, they would." Cliff nodded firmly. "You bake good pies."

A smile tugged at my lips. He was so sure, completely confident we would make enough money to build a rocket to travel to Jupiter, and sure that rocket would work. My shoulders slumped, defeated. "Okay. Tonight I'll ask Dad if he can bring home some peaches."

Cliff jumped up. "Why wait? Let's go find him and ask if we can help bring them home!"

I relished a few more seconds of lying on the grass, the last I might get all summer, then shrugged. "Fine with me."

I followed behind Cliff as he ran into the house yelling, "Mama! Mama! Ma-*ma*!"

"What?" Her voice was slightly muffled, which meant she must have been in the kitchen.

I ran in to find her pulling her hair back into a loose bun; her work clothes were spread over the ironing board. I halted to a stop. "Are you going to the plantation?"

"In a few hours or so. They're ramping up the bed and breakfast for the tourists again. Their first big customer came yesterday, and I wasn't there. So guess what I got?" She made a face. "A talking to, that's what. I swear, they treat me like a child. Or a slave. A slave in their plantation house." She rolled her eyes and picked up a lotion bottle off the counter, pausing to pump lotion onto her smooth white hands. She rubbed her palms together and sighed while reaching for a rag to hold the iron.

Once, when I was hardly five years old, I'd asked Mama why she always put lotion on her hands. She told me that soft, supple hands were a woman's crowning glory.

I looked down at my grass-stained knuckles and hid them behind my back. "Can we go to the peach farm and see Dad? We want to ask for some peaches."

She frowned, a tiny crease appearing on her forehead. "Will you be back in time to make supper? I won't have time to get anything started before I leave."

"Yes, ma'am, I will. I promise."

Since my promises were as good as gold, she let us go, and we raced all the way to the peach farm.

Our feet pounded on the gravel driveway, and I enjoyed the warm, breezy air kissing my windblown cheeks. The houses of our neighborhood whizzed past. By the time we reached the peach farm, our chests were heaving and we kneeled over, gasping for air.

"I beat you," Cliff wheezed.

I rolled my eyes. "Please."

Dad was standing in the middle of the orchard with a pair of pliers in his hands. He looked up, wiping sweat off his forehead, and frowned when he saw us. "What are y'all doing here?"

We ran toward him and swung our legs over the fence, climbing into the orchard. I placed a hand over my brow to shield off the sun. "We wanted to know if we could have some peaches. We're going to use them to make pies and sell the pies for money to build a rocket."

"To Jupiter," Cliff added.

"Yeah." I gave him my best smile, wrapping my arm around Cliff for added sweetness. I tried to read Dad's eyes—would he see how much this crazy plan meant to his son? "Please?"

Dad frowned again and turned back to his work. "I can't give y'all peaches."

Cliff's face fell. "Why not?"

"Well, first off, they're not my peaches. They're Luke Leggett's. And second off, you two don't need to be building rockets and causing trouble. We have enough trouble in the family already," he muttered.

My chest began to swell with disappointment and anger. "It's not causing trouble! I'm a good cook! I know people would buy my pies."

Dad sighed and turned, cupping my cheek. "Scarlett, baby, I know you're a good cook. I just don't need the trouble this summer. If you want to buy the peaches yourself or make money some other way, that's fine. But I can't be troubling Mr. Leggett about it right now." He glanced at his watch and set down the pliers. "Now, I'm heading home. You two run along, okay?" He started for his truck.

"Wait!" Cliff followed on his heels. "I wanna ride in the Clunker."

Dad laughed, and swung into the driver's seat with a teasing smile. "Y'all ran here, didn't you? Well, run on back." His key turned in the ignition and then he was gone, a cloud of dust following behind him.

I watched him go until he was just a speck at the end of the long dirt road that went through our community. "Well, there goes that dream," I muttered, kicking at the driveway. I walked back to the white picket fence and sat on the ground. *What are we going to do now? I'll never get enough money to buy that wood unless I take a job working at the plantation like Mama.* Images of myself dressed in mid-nineteenth-century hoop skirts serving apple pie flashed across my mind. I wrinkled my nose. *Yuck.*

I leaned against the fence to watch the sky again. "At least it's a pretty day. No clouds or anything." I let myself ease down the fence then pulled my knees to my chest and rested my chin on them. "Don't you love the sky in June? It's like cotton candy—smooth and sweet and fluffy. The tinges of pink hidden in the blue …" I sighed. "What do you think, Cliff?"

Silence. I frowned and looked around. "Cliff?"

"Talking to yourself again?"

My skin leapt. I scurried to my feet and whipped around. Frank Leggett was standing in the middle of the orchard watching me. A grin tugged at his mouth. "You seem to do that a lot."

My eyes scanned the orchard. No Cliff in sight. I stood and brushed off my jeans. "This is going to sound really stupid, but have you seen my brother?"

Frank nodded his head. "Isn't he the one stealing peaches?"

"What?" Blood drained from my face. "Where?"

He pointed toward the south side of the orchard. "I saw him over there."

I ran in that direction, my heart pounding along with my feet. *Oh no, Cliff. This is beyond stupid.*

I found him standing under a peach tree, jumping to reach the fruit on the lowest branches. A small pile of peaches already lay at his feet. He brightened when he saw me. "Can you reach that one for me?"

My mouth hung open. I looked from the peaches to him and back to the peaches. "Cliff, what are you doing?"

He shrugged. "Dad will never find out."

"Cliff, you can't *steal* peaches. God will strike you dead or something." I glanced at the sky again.

Frank ran up behind me. "Hey." He nodded at Cliff.

Cliff pressed his lips together in a tight smile and went back to picking peaches. I stood in dumbfounded silence, watching him. *Is he really going to keep stealing them right in front of me and Frank?*

Frank stepped forward and began pulling down fruit from some of the higher branches and dropping it on the ground. "What are all these peaches for?"

My eyes widened. "You can't just help him steal!"

They ignored me.

"Scarlett's gonna sell some peach pies and use the money to build a rocket to Jupiter for me. We hope to finish it by the end of the summer."

Frank nodded, like this was the most normal thing in the world.

And I guess it was sort of normal Cliff-like behavior. But Frank wouldn't have known that.

After several minutes of silent staring, my senses finally began coming back. "What are you doing here?" I asked Frank.

He dropped the rest of the peaches before sticking his hands in his pockets and looking at me. "I live here. Or at least, just up that hill." He pointed. "I was actually on my way over there to … um … take care of a few things, when I saw your brother here and I was curious. And then I heard you talking to yourself again and figured something was up."

I pressed my lips together and asked, "What are *you* planning to do with all these peaches you picked?"

Frank glanced at Cliff. "Well, I thought the kid said you were making peach pies to sell so you can make a rocket."

"So you're giving us these peaches?"

He nodded.

I folded my arms, assuming a defensive position. "For how much?"

A smile tugged at Frank's mouth for the second time that day. "Sometimes people are just nice."

My eyes narrowed. "It's more than that. What?"

The smile turned into a full-out grin, illuminating his face. "Okay, okay. At first I was interested in your arrival because I've always had a crush on your sister, Juli, and I figured y'all could put in a good word for me."

"Juli wouldn't date you in a million years."

He didn't flinch at my bluntness. He only nodded. "Yeah, I know. So now I've decided to help you both because a rocket to Jupiter sounds really fun." He glanced at me. "And I happen to love peach pie and was hoping you'd give me a slice for free."

I shrugged. "I guess."

He continued staring at me with his gold-green eyes. My skin began to heat, a bright red blush creeping over my cheeks. "What?"

He smiled. "You have really messy hair."

Self-conscious, I reached up. The loose ponytail my hair had been tucked into had come undone long ago, and now chunks were hanging around my shoulders in loose waves. I pulled out the hair tie and tucked what I could behind one ear. "We ran here." *I was wrong to grow it out. I should have left it short and neat.*

A teasing glint twinkled in Frank's eye. "You look like a hippie. Like your sister."

I frowned. "I am not a hippie."

He shrugged. "Would you rather I say you looked like a fairy child? Or a runaway princess with briars in her hair? Because I could."

Cliff wrinkled his nose. "I liked hippie better."

Frank smirked. "Me too. Now come on." He stood and brushed off his pants. "Let's take these to the bomb shelter." He scooped up an armful of peaches and began walking down the hill.

What? I grabbed some peaches and scurried after him. "Why are we going to a bomb shelter?"

"No one ever uses it except me," he said over his shoulder. "It's the perfect place to build a rocket."

I watched him from the back. He was tall and thin, with strong arms. His light brown hair was growing lighter in the sunshine, turning the color of golden pancakes. Every couple steps, he'd turn to glance at Cliff to make sure he didn't fall behind.

I wonder if Juli ever had any classes with him. Maybe she could tell me what Frank's like.

"Here we are."

Frank stopped in front of what was indeed an old bomb shelter and dropped the peaches on the ground. "My parents built this in the fifties, but I don't think they ever used it." He pressed his lips together, as if holding back a secret. "Though it hasn't exactly been vacant all this time. I kind of, uh, used it for my own purposes." He stepped forward to open the door and stopped mid-swing. His eyes darted toward us. "Promise not to tell anyone what you see inside."

I smirked. "What are you hiding in there? Nuclear weapons?"

"Ha, ha."

Cliff studied the door in silence. His eyes drifted over toward Frank and looked him over. "We will keep your secrets," Cliff finally declared. "You seem like an *amigo*."

Frank grinned. "Yeah, sure." He pushed open the door and fumbled for a switch. Light flooded the small shelter and revealed quite a sight.

—All kinds of animals filled the room. Birds sat on the rafters, two rabbits munched on newspaper clippings in the corner, a turtle inched its way across the floor, and the furry little heads of kittens peeked out of a box by the door.

"Whoa," Cliff breathed as he stepped inside. "It's like the ark."

I knelt on the floor and stroked the kittens' heads. They were soft and warm, pitifully mewing. "Who do all these animals belong to?"

"Me." Frank closed the door behind us and went to work picking up newspaper shreds off the dirt floor.

My eyebrows rose. "Where did you get them?"

"I rescued most of them. I found those kittens under the porch of an abandoned house last week. It was raining hard, and they were pretty miserable." He picked up a turtle. "I found this outside my bedroom window one morning. He's missing an eye. See?"

The one-eyed reptile recoiled his head into his shell and watched us. Frank reached into the corner. A baby deer sat nestled in a makeshift bed. Frank scooped up the deer and held it in his lap, petting it gently. "This one's pretty special. Her name is Fawn. I found her in the woods behind the house after she hurt her leg during a thunderstorm. Must've tripped over a log or something. Her leg was in a splint for almost a month, but it's still pretty weak. I don't think she'll be able to walk for a few more months, at least." His mouth tilted up in a lopsided smile. "I feed her milk out of a bottle."

I looked around. "Do they all have names?"

Frank shrugged. "Only the ones I intend to keep. Though Fawn here is actually promised to a farmer down the road—said he'd keep her safe and sound in his back pasture once she's healed, since she can't very well go back into the wild. The ones I plan to let go stay nameless. It's too hard to say good-bye to a pet, but it's not as bad to leave a wild animal."

Cliff scrambled on the floor next to me and picked up a kitten, holding it close to his chest. "Do the kittens have names?"

"No. Would you like to name them?" Frank put Fawn back on her bed then pulled an unopened carton of milk from inside a bowl on the shelf and poured it into another bowl. One side of his mouth twitched up. "I keep some on ice for the little guys."

"Hmm …" Cliff studied the tiny black furball in his arms. "I think his name should be Antonio." He pointed to an orange cat in the litter. "And that one's Diego."

Frank raised an eyebrow. "Um, okay."

I lifted a gray kitten from the box. "This one is Mittens." Simple, but suitable. His body heat emanated through my fingertips.

Frank turned and cocked his head. "Yeah. It fits him."

I sat back against the wall and watched Frank pet the kittens. He looked up and asked, "So how many pies are you planning to make? Are you going to make a stand to sell them?" He brightened. "Oh, now that I think about it, I think I have some spare wood behind the shed. I could build you a stand, and Cliff could paint a sign. Would you like that?"

Cliff nodded. "I'm actually pretty good at painting."

Frank looked at me and grinned. Then his smile slowly faded. "What?" he asked.

I frowned and avoided his eye. "I just don't get why you're even talking to us. I don't think I've said more than two sentences to you before today."

He shrugged, rubbing his hands together. "I just felt like it."

I gave him a wry smile. "Are you always so spontaneous?"

Frank nodded. "Yeah. I am." He looked me directly in the eye. "To tell the truth, I've always considered both of you to be a little odd, and I guess you thought I was strange too. So I figured we'd get along fine. And we do."

For some weird reason, it made sense. I guess things were always so offbeat and random with Cliff that anything out of the ordinary seemed normal to me.

Cliff stood and brushed off his jeans. "Oooo-*kay*. If you two are done, I'm going to go get some more peaches." He bolted out of the shelter and disappeared into the orchard.

Frank watched him leave before placing a clinging kitten back on the ground and turning toward me. "Come on. I'll show you that wood."

All kinds of lumber was stacked in the backyard, ranging from large to small, smooth to rough. Frank picked up a sturdy piece of wood and looked it over, chewing on his bottom lip. "Do you think this'll work for the base?"

I shrugged. "You know better than I do. I'll bake the pies, but you and Cliff will have to build the stand yourselves."

He puffed out his cheeks and released the captured air slowly. "Okay. I guess I'll have to teach him how to wield a hammer, huh?"

"Yep."

"And cut wood with a saw?"

I bit my lower lip. "No, I think you'd better do that."

"Scarlett!" Cliff came running around the corner, barely stopping for breath. "Dad just drove by! We have to go home and make supper, remember?"

"Oh, yeah." My brow furrowed. *Drat.*

Frank set the wood back down. "Why don't I come over to your place tomorrow with some of this wood? Cliff can help me make the stand, and you can reward me with one of those delicious pies." He winked.

I grinned. "Sure."

Cliff grabbed my arm and began running back toward home. I followed him, pausing to yell over my shoulder. "Thanks!"

Chapter 4

M rs. Ima Nice sat up as we passed her porch, waving her cane at us. "Hey, you two! Yeah, I'm talking to you!"

Uh-oh. I turned slowly and winced. Her voice was as screechy as nails on a chalkboard and loud enough to keep all the birds away from her window. She was kind of known for the irony of her name. I seemed to recall Mama telling us that Mrs. Nice was called Ima Kilpatrick before she married the stock broker from Vermont. She was from one of the only families with any money that I knew about in southern Georgia, but I supposed that even money couldn't keep you from ending up a leathery, bitter old woman, selling eggs to the neighborhood children. "Yes, ma'am?"

She stiffened her lower lip. "You didn't come for eggs last Tuesday, and I want to know why."

Cliff's foot nudged the back of my heel, pushing me forward. I clutched my hands together, stammering. "Well, uh … I didn't do any baking on Tuesday, and I guess I just sort of forgot. Plus, I normally remember when I'm frying pancakes because I always realize then I'm out of eggs. But last Tuesday Dad went to work early and we just had cereal." My tongue turned numb at the fierce scowl on her face. "And so I forgot."

Mrs. Nice's pale, wrinkled hand clutched her cane as she struggled to stand. "Well, I'll have you know that my chickens—"

Without warning, Cliff turned and bolted, homeward bound. My mouth dropped open. "Cliff!" I shrieked, running after him.

"Come back here, missy!" Mrs. Nice's high-pitched voice could still be heard behind us.

We picked up the pace, our heels sending up miniature dust devils on the road. *Anything to get away from that nightmare of a lady.*

Cliff beat me home by three seconds. We stood by the porch for a few minutes, trying to pull ourselves together before Mama saw us. Cliff pulled a few peach tree leaves out of my hair, and I brushed the dirt off his jeans. "Okay," I finally said, looking Cliff over. "You're pretty clean. I think we're good."

Mama was sitting at the kitchen table paying bills. By now, she was fully dressed in her plantation uniform, her long hair piled on top of her head. Little frown lines covered her forehead. "Oh, great," she mumbled, scribbling something on a piece of paper. She looked up when she saw us come in. "Good, you're back." She started to stand. "Scarlett, I'm getting ready to leave, so I need you to make sure Grandpop Barley gets to bed. Ask Juli if she'll help you clean up the house." She bent to kiss my cheek.

I nodded but made a face so she knew I wasn't happy. She laughed and rubbed my arm. "Oh, and don't let him have any more peanut butter. I found the jar up there in his room today. He's going to eat himself sick." She ruffled Cliff's hair before he had time to duck. "You two be good, okay? Your dad should be back soon. He went to get fuel for the truck." Her keys jingled as she pulled them out and left, slamming the door behind her.

I groaned and banged my head against the refrigerator. I felt like an unappreciated employee, way down in the ranks, who got stuck with the task of running things because no one would.

So running the family fell to me again. I whipped up a quick casserole dish and dished up a plate for Grandpop before trudging up the stairs and knocking on his bedroom door. *Well, here goes.* I popped my head in and saw him sitting in his armchair, flipping through a book. I brightened, forcing a smile onto my face. "Hiya, Grandpop! What are you reading?" Cliff slipped into the room after me with his own plate of casserole.

I stepped forward to drop off Grandpop Barley's dinner, and peeked at the book. The title was upside down. I groaned and turned the book so it was readable then handed it back. "You'll get further this way."

Hands on my hips, I walked out and stood on the top of the stairway, leaning over the railing. *Where's Juli? I didn't hear the door slam so she's got to still be home.*

"Juli!" Silence. I leaned a little further forward. *Whoa!* The railing wobbled beneath me. I recoiled and stepped back, startled. *Remember to have Dad look at that.*

I glanced back at Cliff. He was sitting on the floor of Grandpop Barley's room, blissfully lost in his television show. "You two stay right here, and don't talk to each other. I'll be right back."

Music drifted under the doorway of our bedroom. I knocked on the door. "Juli?"

No answer.

I knocked harder. "Juli! Let me in! Dinner's ready and I need you to help me with the chores."

Still nothing. I pressed my ear to the door, trying to hear inside. I jiggled the knob, but it was locked. "Juli, I know you're in there!"

"Is Mama gone?" Her voice was slow and slurred. I jumped at the sound of it.

"Yeah. Now let me in."

The door opened, and Juli appeared in front of me. Her eyes were lined with kohl, and I noticed the blue streaks were slowly fading from her hair. In her hand, she clutched a large bag. "Okay, I'm out. I'll see you later. Don't tell Mama I'm gone. Tell her I'm in my room or something. Studying."

She brushed past me on wobbling legs, heading down the hall into the kitchen. My eyes widened, unsure of how to deal with such a request, or with the odd behavior of my sister. "Juli, you can't leave. Mama would …" I shook my head. "Mama would not be happy. Besides, I need you to straighten up the living room while I help get Grandpop Barley ready for bed."

She flicked a strand of hair off her shoulder before pausing in the doorway. "See you later, Scarlett." She lifted two fingers and winked. "Peace." Then she disappeared, and I heard a car pulling out of the driveway.

I ran to the window. Ziggy was sitting in the driver's seat of a beat-up yellow Volkswagen. Juli hopped in the passenger's seat and threw her bag in the back before they drove away.

I shook my head and shuddered. *Mama will be worse than not happy.*

Shouts erupted upstairs. My head began to hurt. *What now?*

I bounded up the steps. "Get your hands off of that, you filthy child!" Grandpop Barley was shouting.

"Hey, let go!"

I burst open the door. Cliff and Grandpop Barley were on the floor, wrestling over a jar of peanut butter. My mouth dropped open. "What on earth?"

With his toothless mouth foaming, Grandpop Barley took a swing at Cliff. "Let go of my peanut butter," he growled.

"You're not allowed to eat it!" Cliff protested, ducking the attacks. He looked up and caught sight of me standing in the doorway. "Scarlett! Tell him he's not allowed to eat it!"

I moved toward the skirmish while trying to clear my head. "Okay, both of you get off each other! You're acting like a couple of toddlers." I wrenched Cliff away from Grandpop Barley and placed him firmly on the ground. Then I gripped Grandpop Barley's arm and led him back to his armchair. "Sit."

I stood back and looked at the two of them. My eyes wandered to the abandoned jar of peanut butter on the ground. *That will only cause more trouble.* I picked it up and hid it behind my back. I frowned at Grandpop Barley, wagging my finger at him like a child. "If you keep carrying on like this, Mama will never let you have any peanut butter."

He muttered to himself, wrapping his arms around his chest and glaring at Cliff. "Troublesome kid tried to take it from me. He wanted it for himself."

"Did not." Cliff stuck out his tongue. "Grandpop Barley *knew* he wasn't allowed to have it. He told me not to let Mama know."

"Okay, okay." I placed a hand on my forehead. *Why do I always have to fix everything?* I pointed at Cliff. "You go downstairs and play with your cans. I'll be down in a little while. And you ..." I glanced at Grandpop Barley. "I am going to give you a bath, so you go into the bathroom and wait for me," I said firmly, "while I go throw away this peanut butter."

"Throw it away?" Grandpop Barley sat up, his eyes suddenly looking very sad. Tears welled up in the corners of them as he stared at the container. "But it's such a nice jar." The tips of his moustache sagged downward. "I love that jar."

My heart pinched with guilt, but I was resolved to stay strong. "Yes, it is, but you behaved very badly, and I'm afraid that means I have to throw this peanut butter away." I hid it behind my back, where he couldn't see it anymore. I hated treating him like this, but it seemed to be the only way he responded nowadays. "Here," I said, lifting his red necktie. "I'll wash this tomorrow and give it back to you."

"No!" His eyes turned wild. He clutched at the tie, trying to grab it from my hands. "Give it to me!"

I recoiled. "No way. It smells like sweaty peanut butter."

"It's mine!"

I shook my head. "This tie hasn't been washed in months. It's disgusting."

Grandpop Barley lurched forward and snatched it from me, holding it to his chest. "It's *mine.*"

I took a step back. He was foaming at the mouth again, his face turning a tomato-ish shade of red against his pale skin. "Okay," I said slowly. "You can keep it. Never mind about the bath. Now, just … go to bed."

After I'd put Cliff down for the night and grabbed some dinner for myself, I sat in my room and looked through cookbooks until I heard the kitchen door open downstairs and could make out the faint voices of Mama and Dad. I shut the cookbooks and tucked them under my arm. My shadow loomed on the floor in front of me.

I made my way down the stairs, my shoulders heavy. *I'd better tell Mama about Cliff and Grandpop Barley's fight.*

The voices in the kitchen were getting louder. I could make out a few words. They were talking about money. Bills, checks, loans … Dad was sounding angrier, while Mama's voice was starting to break.

I placed the cookbooks on a bookshelf in the living room and made my way to the kitchen. A door slammed and Dad stormed out toward his bedroom. I pushed open the kitchen door and stuck my head inside. No one.

Muffled sobs were audible from the bathroom. I tiptoed across the floor and pressed my ear against the door. Hesitating, I whispered, "Mama?"

A sniff. And then, "What is it, dear?"

My heart began to race. "Is everything okay?"

Mama was silent for several seconds. "Yes," she finally replied, her voice soft and paper-thin. "Everything's fine. Was there something you needed?"

I thought about telling her about Cliff and Grandpop Barley but decided not to. "No." I turned to go.

"Scarlett?" she called.

"Yes?"

"Is … is Juli home?" She sounded quiet and scared, like a little girl.

I lowered my eyes, pressing my head against the door. Mama sniffed. My chest squeezed. "Yes," I lied. "She's in our room."

"Good."

I went to my room alone, stopping to check on Cliff. He was sleeping soundly, undisturbed by the drama downstairs. I envied him; my heart was beating hard. I'd heard Mama crying and told a lie. Something told me both of those things weren't right.

I crawled into bed and wished I was a little kid again and could sleep all through the night without any cares or worries. I closed my eyes and took a deep breath. *Tomorrow will be better.*

● ● ●

The next morning, I slept in until almost eight. Then I rubbed my eyes and stretched, feeling the warm sun shining on my face through the window. My bed was so warm and snuggly. I pulled the covers up to my chin and sighed, feeling happy and ready to start over again. *Another day. Another morning.* A smile spread across my face. *And isn't it lovely?*

Juli's bed was rumpled. *So she did come home last night.*

A hammer pounded outside, disturbing my state of sleepy elation. *What on earth?* It was too early for Dad to be home on his work break.

I pushed the covers off and stood, holding back a gasp when my bare feet hit the cold wood floor. I scrunched up my toes and stretched before heading downstairs.

Voices sounded from inside the house. I bounded down the steps and squinted. "What's that noise?" I ran into the kitchen and froze.

Frank Leggett stood in the open doorway, hammer in hand. He

was laughing at something Cliff just said. They both looked up when I stepped in.

"Oh. Good morning, Scarlett."

I could feel Frank's eyes look me up and down, from my bare feet to my rumpled pajamas. A smile tugged at his mouth. "You have really messy hair."

I crossed my arms, my face heating. "Thanks for pointing that out again. As if I didn't notice."

Cliff stuck out a gray mass of fur. "Frank brought Mittens over when he came to help build the pie stand."

Oh, right. Frank said he was coming in the morning. My face flushed all over again.

"Hey, want to hear a knock-knock joke?" Cliff asked, turning to Frank.

Frank stepped into the house and shrugged. "Sure."

"Knock, knock."

"Who's there?" A tiny grin pulled at Frank's mouth; he was expecting a good joke. That made me feel good for some reason. He didn't think Cliff was stupid. He thought Cliff was the kind of kid who could make up a good punch line.

"Nobel."

"Nobel who?"

"No bell at all, that's why I had to knock."

They both laughed, and I remembered that I was standing on the edge of the kitchen in my pajamas.

"Well." I crossed the kitchen and opened the refrigerator, pulling out a carton of orange juice. I poured it into a glass, avoiding their eyes. "If you give me a few minutes to dress, I'll come out to help you."

"We'll wait." Frank eyed the carton and pulled up a chair. "I might take some of that while I'm sitting here."

I rolled my eyes and handed him my untouched glass. "Just take this. I'll be right back."

I took the steps two at a time, running into my bedroom. *What to wear ...* I pulled out a worn pair of blue jeans and a gingham shirt, pulling them over my narrow body. I glanced at myself in the mirror. *My hair.*

It really was wild—a zigzagging mess of auburn falling all around my shoulders. I grimaced at the thought of brushing it. *It just becomes big and poufy, and that really is ten times worse than ratty.* Plus, messy hair is ten times worse when you have freckly skin. I'm sure the porcelain-skinned girls can pull off any type of hairstyle. Those of us with freckles and dimples have to work a little harder. And then there was that little birthmark by my mouth ...

I sighed. *I'm not even going to think about that thing this morning.*

Finally, I settled on running a comb through the snarls before pulling my hair into a ponytail. Then I threw on some tennis shoes and ran back downstairs.

Frank and Cliff were still sitting at the table discussing the Spanish Civil War. "It really was unfortunate," Cliff said, taking a sip of juice, "that so many Spaniards should die." He grinned. "I have a real affection for the Spanish culture."

Frank raised an eyebrow. "So I've noticed."

I cleared my throat, and they both looked up. "I'm ready."

● ● ●

Cutting wood was hard work. It was heavy and splintery, and the Georgia heat was already growing unbearable. Not that Cliff and I were much help. We lifted a piece of lumber here and there and helped hammer a few nails. But mostly we sat atop piles of wood and sipped lemonade while watching Frank work.

He was really strong for a skinny boy of seventeen. I guess working at his father's peach farm built his strength somehow. Cliff poked at his own muscles, probably hoping that under his scrawny arms was the same amount of strength.

"Frank?" I asked after a while.

"Yeah?" He glanced up, squinting from the sun.

"Are you smart?"

He made a face. "What kind of a question is that?"

I swung my legs, thinking through the question. "Well, you seem to know a lot about math. Or at least about shapes and angles. You know, for building the stand." I bit my lip. "But everyone knows you do poorly in school. I mean, not that I do much better … Because … I don't … do much better, I mean. Well, I do get slightly better grades. But still …" My face warmed, and instantly I wanted to grab all my words and stuff them back into my mouth. "You know what I mean."

Frank smiled. Apparently, I couldn't offend him, no matter how hard I seemed to be trying. He propped up a piece of wood and leaned against it. "I rescue kittens. And turtles. I read about gravitational force and perpetual motion for fun. No one talks to me at school, so I pretty much live in my own little world. How much more of a dweeb would people consider me if I pulled straight As?"

"That's really smart," Cliff quipped, beaming at Frank.

Frank chuckled. "Thanks." He turned and continued nailing boards together.

I wanted to say what was on my mind, but I didn't. I wanted to tell him that it didn't matter what people thought—that he should do well in school and not be ashamed of it. Frank was good-looking and smart and actually really sweet. It didn't make any sense that he would worry about protecting himself from others' opinions. But maybe it was different when you were alone. At least I always had Cliff. The only creatures Frank had to talk to were turtles and rabbits.

"Here. I think it's finished." Frank stood back and admired his work.

It was about five feet long with room for two wide shelves on the front. Four posts flanked the corners of the counter to allow for a canopy overhead. And there was just enough room in back for three chairs.

"It's perfect."

Cliff ran up and stood behind the stand. "I get to paint the sign. I'll hang it right here." He pointed, practically puffed up with joy.

Pressing a hand to my back, I faked a heavy sigh. "I guess you guys deserve a homemade peach pie. Might as well throw one together for you, seeing as I'm so appreciative and everything." I winked at them both and headed back into the house.

Chapter 5

The kitchen was hot and sticky, filled with the smell of baking pies. I inspected the center of the pies looking for gooey, bubbly bits. *Not quite ready yet.* I stepped back and closed the oven door.

"How's it coming?"

I spun around. Frank stood behind me with his hands in his pockets. "Sorry." He looked at me sheepishly. "Where's Cliff?"

I pushed a strand of hair behind my ear. "I think he's in the living room looking at his Spanish dictionary." Frank opened his mouth, but I held up my hand. "Don't even ask."

He laughed, looking around the kitchen. "What a wreck. Do you need help cleaning up?"

I shrugged. "Sure." I set to work scrubbing the counter. Peachy streaks had stained the wood. I grimaced. *Mama isn't going to be too happy about this.*

Frank began piling dishes in the sink and running hot water. He glanced at me. "Why do you wear your apron inside out?"

I looked down, and my face reddened. I hadn't realized it was still like this. I pulled the apron off and turned it right-side out. It was white and lacy, with the initials *VB* written in fancy script across the chest. "It's Mama's. Her mother gave it to her as a wedding gift. Mama passed it on to me a few years ago because she stopped cooking, but I couldn't bear to get it dirty. It's too beautiful."

I flipped the apron so Frank could see the back again. It was covered with stains and streaks—everything from red sauce to chocolate. "I'm not the neatest cook."

He laughed. "That's a really good idea." He dug around in the soapy water, scrubbing a dirty pan. "It would be a shame if anything would happen to that apron. Although the back of it is already so dirty … I suppose it wouldn't hurt to …" A second later he flung a handful of soapy water at me and the apron.

I squealed and ducked, shielding the apron. "Hey!" Warm water splattered on my cheek and my jeans. I picked up the sponge I was using and threw it at him.

Soon, the full-fledged water war was on. We were laughing and ducking and spewing soapy water at each other. Cliff heard and ran in. Grabbing a sponge, he joined the ruckus. I squeezed my eyes shut, soap stinging at my lashes. Blindly, I continued to splash water. And then, just as suddenly as it started, the laughter stopped. My eyes flew open and settled on Juli standing in the corner of the kitchen.

Her mouth was twisted in a sardonic grin. Today she was wearing a long skirt and had a headband-ish thing tied around her head. Still pretty, still hippie. She looked us over, then her eyes slowly trailed across the room—from the soapy counters to the slippery floor to our drenched hair. Then she raised an eyebrow. "Make peace, not war." She rolled her eyes and trailed out of the kitchen, slamming the screen door. Her boyfriend's laugh sounded through the yard as he started up his Volkswagen and pulled out of the driveway.

Frank was still staring at the closed door. "I've been wondering for a while … What's with the blue hair?"

I shrugged. "She's not into 'conforming to the age.'"

His eyes were wide. "Incredible."

It sent little shivers up my spine to think about Frank pining for my sister. Juli, with the raccoon eyes and streaky blue hair and hippie boyfriend. My stomach churned. "Well, the color's almost gone anyway. She gave up on it after a while." I licked my lips and rubbed my hands on the corner of my apron. "Hey, let's get this kitchen cleaned up for real this time."

Frank blinked and nodded. "Yeah, sure."

• • •

Supper that night was pretty quiet. Juli was home, picking at her peas and complaining that she couldn't eat beef because of her new diet.

"It's called *vegan*, Dad. Some people actually prefer it."

He rolled his eyes and took a large bite. "It's called *ridiculous*. God made meat for mankind to eat, not to picket for."

Juli bristled. "Well, you just wouldn't understand, would you?"

He glanced at her sharply. "Watch it."

She lowered her eyes, her back still rigid.

Mama glanced around the table and grimaced. Cliff was staring down at his plate, quietly counting his peas, while I pretended to be fascinated by the salt shaker. Grandpop Barley was poking his fork into the table, smiling at the little dimples it left in the wood. "Dad." Mama's voice was strained. "Please ... don't."

He frowned and dropped his fork, crossing his arms instead.

I gazed up and saw Mama and Dad exchange a look. Then Mama brightened and turned to me.

"Scarlett, I ran across Dotty Greene in the grocer's today, and she asked if you could be spared one day a week to cook supper for the church's shut-ins. The Greenes have a wonderfully stocked kitchen—everything you'll need to prepare a nice meal. And Dotty seemed so eager to have you over to teach her a thing or two about cooking. Poor thing, they never really got past the honeymoon stage, it seems. I think she's a little stuck." Mama took a bite of meat, chewing carefully. "I told her you'd be more than happy to help her. You're going every Friday from three to seven, starting tomorrow."

My mouth dropped open. "You told her that without asking me?"

Mama raised her brows. "Honey, what else do you have to do?"

I held my chin up, indignant. "Well, I have a lot of stuff to do this summer. We're running a pie stand every Saturday, and I've got things to bake and, well, I've got to sell them and ..."

Mama cut me off. "Oh, Scarlett, surely you can spare a few hours one day a week. Don't be so melodramatic." She glanced at Juli. "It's not healthy."

I pressed my lips together, willing myself not to say anything more. She wouldn't listen anyway.

Cliff began humming to himself. He looked down and picked at the dirt caked on his bitten nails. Then he glanced up with excited eyes. "Hey, can we play charades after supper?"

Dad shook his head. "Your mom and I are going to a political meeting. It's very important. These darned politicians—always trying to tell us what to do. Someone's got to say something."

Mama reached out and placed her soft hand on his arm, calming him. "Save it for the meeting, Bill."

"Well ..." Juli pushed away from the table. "I'm leaving. Peace." She saluted us and brushed out of the kitchen.

"Hey, wait!" Dad stood. "Where are you going?"

The screen door slammed. Silence fell over the table. I poked my hand with my fork and winced. Dad's chest deflated. He picked up his half-eaten plate of food and glanced at Mama. "Well, we better get going. We don't want to get there after it's started."

● ● ●

The house seemed so quiet once they were gone. Cliff, Grandpop Barley, and I sat in the living room in silence. Cliff was messing with an old toy airplane, examining it for possible ideas for fuel tanks and engines. Grandpop Barley sat near the fireplace, stroking his red tie. And I lay on the couch, watching them both. It was such a sad picture—both of them sitting so close, yet so disinterested in the other.

"Well," I finally said, pulling myself up. "Are you ready?"

Cliff's eyes darted toward me, a glimmer of hope in them. "Ready for what?"

I shrugged. "To play charades. Who says we need Mama or Dad?"

He leaped to his feet then bounced on the balls of his toes, swaying back and forth. "Yes! I'm ready! I'm ready!"

I crossed over to the old gramophone and flipped through the records in the cabinet. I wondered if my parents had ever heard of the modern record player. *Probably not.* I blew the dust off an old record and grinned. *The Diamonds.* I placed it on the turntable and cranked the handle. *Perfect. A little doo-wop to get things started.* Peppy music filled the speakers, flooding the room with sunshine. I glanced at Grandpop Barley. "Are you ready?"

He grunted. Didn't sound like he ever would be.

Oh, well. Two's better than one. I stood in the center of the living room. "Okay, now you have to guess what I am. Are you ready?"

"Yes!"

I laughed and began strutting around the room. I flapped my arms out, pushing my head back and forth. My tail-end wiggled along with the tiny steps I took.

Cliff sat up straight. "A chicken!"

"Right!" I collapsed on the couch. "Your turn."

"Okay." He stood in the center of the room, suddenly looking shy. "Um, what should I do?"

"Anything!" I laughed and threw a pillow at him. "Just come on!"

"Oh, I got it!" He grabbed the pillow and made a big show out of holding it in his arms. He began walking around, touching the pillow somewhat awkwardly. With a large sigh, Cliff kissed the pillow and pretended to pinch it. His face scrunched up into a funny look I guessed was meant to be adoration.

I pressed my lips together, holding in my laughter. "Could it be your sweetheart? Has Cliff Blaine finally found true love?"

"Ew, gross!" He made a face.

I wiggled my eyebrows. "Are you proposing marriage? Who's the lucky lady?"

This time, Cliff thrust the pillow to his shoulder and patted it. Hard. "It's crying," he explained, clearly annoyed.

My eyes widened in mock confusion. "Why, I have no idea!"

"What?" That must have been the last straw. Cliff dropped the pillow and stormed toward me.

I couldn't hold back my smile anymore. "Okay, okay. It was a baby. You're the daddy. I get it."

Exasperated, Cliff threw his hands in the air. "Yes! Finally!" He plopped down on the couch. "Your turn."

"Okay, okay …" I stood, still laughing. "Guess this one." I began to spin around the living room ungracefully. I twirled and sashayed, waving my arms around above my head.

"Jumpin' Jehoshaphat!" Grandpop Barley suddenly leaped to his feet and threw a pillow at me.

The pillow landed squarely in my forehead, sending me to the floor in shcok. Cliff squealed and ran to help me. "Grandpop Barley!" I squeaked, climbing to me feet. *What on earth? And what's up with the pillows tonight?*

The veins were bulging out of his neck. He threw his red tie over his shoulder and wagged a finger at me. "You're doing the devil's dance, Scarlett, and I won't have it! I won't have it! Not in my household!" He shook his head. "Not in my household!"

Devil's dance? What kind of religious mumbo-jumbo was *that*? I couldn't remember ever hearing that Grandpop Barley was against dancing. I doubted he even knew what I was imitating. I chewed the side of my lip. Maybe his mind was getting worse. He was losing more marbles in the brain department, that's for sure.

"No, she's not! She's a ballerina!" Cliff protested.

I shook my head, cutting him off. "Okay, Grandpop." Afraid to touch him, I reached one hand out and gently grasped his arm, leading him back to the couch. "Why don't we sit down for a while? Would you like to guess a charade?"

He grumbled under his breath and glared at us from behind bushy eyebrows. But he nodded and crossed his arms. "I suppose. But it better be respectable."

"Um, okay. Respectable, Cliff."

Cliff stood in the middle of the room, clearly still shaken. He took a deep breath and dropped onto his knees. Raising his head to the ceiling fan, he pretended to howl.

"Well, that's easy," Grandpop Barley said gruffly. "He's a dog."

"Good job!"

Cliff stood and started to applaud. "Bravo!"

Grandpop Barley's face turned apple red, but his lips twitched slightly. "Bah!"

Seeing his half-smile, my face blossomed into a full grin, and I settled back on the ground next to Cliff. "Why don't we play a card game or something now?" No use getting Grandpop Barley all fired up like that again.

• • •

"Don't be nervous."

I glanced at Mama. "I'm not nervous."

She raised an eyebrow. "Okay. Go on, ring the doorbell."

The house in front of me was white and clean. Very clean, like it belonged to the type of couple who scrubbed and bleached every inch. Red hydrangeas surrounded the steps, and climbing morning glories wrapped around the porch. A small white swing with two floral cushions hung from the edge of the porch. And suspended above the doorway was an engraved wooden plaque that read "God Bless This Home."

The pastor's home. A sinking feeling grew in my stomach. *What if I spill something? What if I say something rude? What if ...?*

"Scarlett, why aren't you ringing the doorbell?"

Oh, right. I walked up the steps, careful not to touch the clean stair rail. My finger hesitated only a moment before pressing the bell. It sounded from within the house like a cheery death knell. Footsteps clattered, and then the door flew open.

Mrs. Dotty Greene stood smiling at us. "Oh, do come in! I'm so glad your mother could spare you. I've heard so much about your cooking skills."

Mama waved from the sidewalk. "I'll be back for her at seven."

"Oh, nonsense!" Mrs. Greene shook her head. "I'll walk her home after we deliver the meals. Have a great day."

She shooed me inside and shut the door. The inside of the house was as quaint and sweet as the exterior. The walls were painted pale shades of robin's egg blue, lemony yellow, and mint green. Framed floral prints lined the walls, along with black-and-white photos. The rooms were small and crammed together, but every door was open, leading from one room to another.

"Come into the kitchen." Mrs. Greene opened a closet and pulled out two aprons, tossing one to me. "I'll show you what I'm thinking about making for supper tonight."

I took the apron and turned it inside out before tying it around my waist. Mrs. Greene raised an eyebrow. "Habit," I explained before she could ask.

She shrugged and opened the pantry. "Do you know how to make fried chicken?"

"Of course." *Anyone could do that.*

"Oh, right. You probably do it all the time." She grinned at my indignant face. "I also assume you know how to make buttermilk biscuits, butter beans, and cherry tarts."

I ran the list through my head. "Yes, but I don't know the recipes by heart."

"Oh, don't worry. I have a cookbook. I just can't seem to navigate it very well without a captain."

Mrs. Greene put on her apron. It was difficult for her to get her tall beehive through the small opening. Her blonde hair was always so coiffed and old-fashioned, even though she couldn't have been over thirty.

I wonder if her hair is stiff, like wood. My fingers itched to find out. *Must resist temptation.*

"Okay, let's start with the fried chicken." Mrs. Greene bit her lip. "Now, we've a bit of a challenge with this one."

I frowned. "What do you mean?"

"Well …" Mrs. Greene exhaled heavily. "Do you know Mrs. Ima Nice? She, um, *presented* me with one of her chickens as a gift last week. I couldn't say no, but now I don't know what to do with it. I figured we could use it for the supper."

My mouth dropped open. "A live chicken? We're going to use a *live* chicken?"

"You mean you haven't done it before?" A worry line creased Mrs. Greene's perfectly smooth forehead.

"Of course not! The only chicken I've ever touched is the frozen variety from the grocery store."

Her eyes widened. "I thought everyone around here killed live chickens!"

I made a face. "Maybe some people, but not my family. I know I could never buy a chicken and then cut off its head." The thought made my stomach churn.

Mrs. Greene grimaced. "I didn't buy it. It was a gift. Mrs. Nice said the chicken's name is Mildred." She wrung her hands in her apron. "Oh, at least help me try, Scarlett."

I sighed. "Where is the chicken?"

"Out here." She opened the side door.

A makeshift wire pen surrounded the yard. In the center was a small wooden coop with a large hen clucking and walking around. Dirt clung to its snowy white feathers.

Well, here goes. Taking a deep breath, I ventured out into the yard and attempted to grab the chicken. It jumped away from me, ruffling its feathers. I grimaced and chased it around the coop before finally scooping it up in my arms. Its sharp talons clawed at my chest. I held it away from me, dangling it upside down.

"Here we are."

Mrs. Greene was chewing away her lower lip, clutching the door knob. "How do you suppose we should kill it?"

The chicken cackled at us, obviously disliking the subject. I squirmed. "Well, we could cut off its head."

"In my *kitchen*?"

"We could do it in the yard."

She glanced to her neighbors on the right and left and winced.

I racked my brain. How did people usually kill chickens? "Or we could wring its neck."

Mrs. Greene slid her eyes shut and took a deep breath. I guess that didn't sound much more appealing. I didn't blame her. I wasn't exactly thrilled at the idea of wringing a bird's neck and hearing it crack. Ick.

I groaned. "Why do we have to kill it anyway?"

Her eyes flew open. "Well, what else am I going to do with it?" Her voice grew hot. "I am not going to let that chicken sit around and dirty up my yard and take up space, if that's what you're thinking. This chicken is going to die, and we are going to be resourceful and give it to the shut-ins for supper." She stepped back and grabbed a butcher knife. "And we'll do it in the yard."

Mrs. Greene led me to a tree stump in the middle of the lawn. I placed the chicken on the stump. The dirty bird settled into a comfortable position, finally happy.

My heart flopped. *Poor little ...* "Its name is Mildred," I suddenly whispered, glancing at Mrs. Greene. "Isn't that what Mrs. Nice said?" *Poor little Mildred. Such a short life, ending with such a grievous tragedy.*

Mrs. Greene sighed. "Don't look while I do this if you think you're going to be sick."

I squeezed my eyes shut and braced myself. A thought crossed my mind: *Wasn't I supposed to be the one teaching her how to cook? And here I am standing with my eyes squeezed shut in the middle of her yard.* I heard the swish of the metal as Mrs. Greene raised the knife and then ...

I screamed. The sound of it hitting wood.

The bird squawked. I peeked. *How could it have ...?*

It was still there. Perfectly unharmed. Simply ruffling its feathers angrily at Mrs. Greene and squawking.

"What? But I thought ..."

Mrs. Greene gave a weak smile and held up the butcher knife. It was unstained by blood. She pointed at a notch in the wood. "It had a name." She shrugged and put the knife down. "You can't kill something that has a name."

I stared at the bird, unable to blink. *It's alive!* My heart surged. *It's alive, and I love it!*

Possessed by a sudden rush of happiness, I reached out and hugged Mrs. Greene. "Oh, I'm so glad you didn't kill it!"

She sighed, wringing her apron. "Well, now what are we going to do with it?"

"Oh." My heart sank. It couldn't stay in her perfect yard, lonely and hungry and exposed. I knelt on the ground and watched the hen jump off the stump and peck at some leftover kernels of corn. "I know!" I jumped up. "I have a friend who rescues animals. I'm sure he'll have room for Mildred."

"Okay. We'll take her over there after we've delivered supper. Now, come on. I think I've got some more chicken in the refrigerator—of the frozen variety."

Chapter 6

I watched Mrs. Greene out of the corner of my eye as I rolled out the dough for the cherry tarts. She dropped floured chicken into the frying pan, oblivious of the grease splattering on her clean apron.

"You know"—I cleared my throat—"I never thought I'd be here cooking in your kitchen."

"Well, I'm glad to have you here." She grinned and went back to flipping chicken.

I nodded. "I just always thought … well, you're the preacher's wife. And I was never really sure what to think of you. Because …" I blushed. "Well, Mama says there's such a thing as being too honest."

Mrs. Greene laughed, a full, hearty sound. "Well, my mama told me differently. Never be afraid to say what's on your mind. Be kind, be polite, but be honest." She rubbed her forehead, leaving a greasy black streak. "Lies are always ugly, and there is nothing you can do to make any beauty out of them. But you can take something honest—imperfect, maybe, but still honest—and make something wonderfully beautiful."

Something tickled in my chest. I grinned. "Well, I used to think you were strange and overly perfect, but now I think you're nice."

Mrs. Greene nodded. "And I used to think you and your brother were odd and mischievous and darling, and I still think you are odd and mischievous and darling."

"Thanks." My flour-covered hands pressed out the dough, rolling it into small tart shells. "You should drop by our stand tomorrow. Cliff and I are selling peach pies every Saturday to make enough money to build a rocket."

"Really? Why a rocket?"

I placed the cherries over the cream cheese–based filling I'd already spooned into the tart shells. The summer heat always brought out the fruity sweetness, and my mouth was already watering. "Cliff wants to be the first person on Jupiter."

"He sounds like quite the boy."

"He is. He's smart and funny and sweet." My face glowed. "He can be really strange and obnoxious sometimes, but I really love him."

"He's lucky to have you as a sister."

I looked up from the dough and smiled. "He's my best friend."

"Ah." Something sparked in Mrs. Greene's eyes. She looked down and flipped the chicken out of the pan onto a plate to dry. "Tim and I want children. I think I'd like to have a daughter and son just like you two."

I squirmed. It felt so weird to hear the esteemed Pastor Timothy Greene referred to so casually. In our home, his name was always synonymous with warnings and punishments. As in, *Remember what Pastor Greene said last Sunday …*

"Well, I have an older sister too. Juli. She hasn't been to church very many times, so I'm not sure if you'd know her."

"The girl with blue hair?"

"Well, it's not always blue. Normally, it's a golden brown."

"Interesting." Mrs. Greene eyed my hair. "Your hair has such reddish tones."

I nodded. "Mama was a blonde; Dad was a redhead. Juli just got to split the difference."

"I see." Another piece of chicken sizzled as it landed in the frying pan. "And what's your sister like?"

For some reason, the words to describe Juli escaped my mind. I didn't really think of the way she was now—shabby, wild, and reckless. I could only think of her three years earlier. That Juli was lovely and clean and sparkling.

"Juli has always been very beautiful. She's much prettier than me. In the summer, her hair turns light brown with blonde streaks. It's beyond lovely." Pink and gold evening sunlight streamed into the room. I pinched the crusts of the tarts. "She has a beautiful singing voice, and she used to love country music. Johnny Cash was her favorite because she thought he was not only talented, but also really dreamy looking."

Mrs. Greene nodded. "Tim has a few of his albums."

"I think we still have some of my sister's in a box somewhere." My forehead scrunched up. "Anyway, Juli liked to sing along, and we all enjoyed it. She used to say she was going to be a singer when she grew up. Maybe she still will. I don't really know her anymore."

Mrs. Greene glanced at me. She wiped her hands off on her apron and leaned against the counter. "Now, I'm going to ask you to be honest, Scarlett. What is your sister like lately?"

I lowered my eyes. "Different," I muttered.

She nodded, waiting for me to go on. When I remained silent, she pulled a picnic basket out of the cupboard. "Well, people change. Not just some people. Everyone. You either change for the better or for the worse." She held up the basket. "Do you think this will be big enough?"

I nodded and began placing the already-baked batch of cherry tarts into the basket.

"Your sister is at a very impressionable age right now. And so are you. These are the years that determine what kind of person you are going to be." She shut the lid of the basket and tapped her fingers on the rim. "Just something to think about."

My fingers fiddled with the ties of my apron. "How old are you?"

My face immediately flushed. It was such a rude question. *Mama would beat me with a spoon if she was here.* And yet I didn't take it back. I really wanted to know.

She laughed in surprise. "Twenty-seven. Why do you ask?"

I shrugged. "It's just hard to imagine grown-ups ever being sixteen."

A soft wind blew in from the open window, lifting the stray hairs from Mrs. Greene's beehive. She smiled. "Sometimes it's hard to remember being sixteen." She sighed and leaned against the sink, tapping a wooden spoon to her cheek. "Let's see, when I was sixteen, I was carefree and wild too. I had long blonde hair that stretched to my waist. I keep it a bit shorter now." She touched her piled-up hair. "Tim likes it long, but it gets in my way sometimes."

I watched her green eyes dance. *How could I have ever thought she was lifeless and dull?*

She bit her lip. "I was awfully bad and wild. I think I said that already." She shrugged. "I might have never changed if I hadn't met Tim." A smile pulled at her lips. "He was a student at the local seminary. His father was good friends with the pastor of our church. So when Tim came to town, my parents offered our house to him for the first year of his classes."

"And you fell in love."

Mrs. Greene's eyebrows flew up. "Oh, not at first. At first, I hated him. He was so pious and polite and good all the time. I had a serious beau, anyway. I was rarely at home. But that winter I caught the flu and was on my back for two weeks. Tim offered to read to me in the evenings. I think that's what I first fell in love with—the way he read. His voice is so rich and ... well, you've heard it at church, obviously." She blushed.

I nodded. "He does have a nice voice."

"Right. Anyway, Tim sometimes read out of the Bible. For the first time, I heard about sin and God and our need for repentance.

God brought all kinds of sins to my mind. Times I'd been disobedient or rebellious toward my family and others. It all sank in—how far from Him I was and how there was no chance for forgiveness apart from His grace. I mean, I'd heard it in church, but I guess things just stick with you more when you're flat on your back." She laughed.

"Whatever the reason was, I know now that sickness was from God, because that winter I turned from my sins and trusted Christ for salvation. And I also fell in love with Tim. We married four years later, when I was twenty." She twisted the ring on her finger.

I rubbed a flour-coated hand across my cheek. Dough covered my apron. "That was a nice story."

Mrs. Greene glanced at the clock. "Yes, but we're running late. Thanks for helping me with that second batch of tarts for me and Tim. I'll get those in the oven once you've gone home." She pulled off her apron. "Come on, let's get these delivered to the shut-ins, and we can come back for Mildred later."

● ● ●

With a firm hand, I knocked on Frank's door and stepped back. No answer. Mildred squawked, squirming in my arms. I glanced at Mrs. Greene. "Maybe they're not home."

She shrugged. "Try again."

I had just lifted my hand for the second knock when the door flew open.

Mrs. Leggett stood in the doorway staring at me and my risen hand. Her blonde hair was long and rumpled, and a cigarette hung from her lips.

I lowered my hand to my side and tried not to stare at her nose.

Mrs. Leggett had a reputation like no other in the county, all because of one Christmas vacation. In December of 1967, she went to visit her sister in New York and came back with a different nose. The new nose was long and thin—much different from the short, bumpy one she had before. I'd heard Mama say it was a new type of surgery, but I couldn't recall anyone actually mentioning it to Mrs. Leggett herself. And so we children were instructed to simply not look at her nose.

It was really, really hard.

"Well, darling, what are you doing here?" Mrs. Leggett lifted the cigarette and blew out a puff of smoke. She glanced at the chicken in my arms but was clearly unfazed. I wondered if wild animals were constantly finding their way to her doorstep.

"I'd like to see Frank, if you don't mind. I have a gift for him."

Mrs. Leggett's eyebrows rose. She straightened, looking again at Mildred. "A gift? Oh, how lovely. Do come in, darling. Make yourself at home."

She opened the door and led us in. I stood in the foyer, holding the squirming chicken and trying not to mess up anything. Everything was white. The ceilings, the furniture, the linens. Except for one black wall, standing out starkly against the general whiteness of the living room. There was a whole lot of crystal everywhere. Great potential for a chicken-related disaster.

Mrs. Greene was clearly bothered by the possibility of danger. She pulled off her pristine white gloves. "My, what a lovely home. You have great taste in decorating."

Mrs. Leggett shrugged, one of the sleeves of her silk robe sliding off her shoulder. "Thanks."

"Why, might I ask, did you decide to paint that wall black?"

Mrs. Leggett took another puff of her cigarette. "Why not?"

I stepped around a chair into a small cleared area. "Why is this spot empty?"

"Oh, this is my cha-cha corner." Mrs. Leggett brightened and placed her cigarette on top of the television. "Watch, darling." She leaned over and flipped on an old record. Swinging music filled the room. "Step back, please."

I walked around a pristine white sofa and watched her from a window seat. She began to sway her hips, dancing back and forth. She threw back her head and began moving her arms, screeching, "Chicoooo! Cha-cha-cha!"

Someone bounded down the stairs, and then Frank was standing in the doorway of the parlor with a look of horror on his face. "Mother!"

"Oh, Frank, darling, would you turn up that record?" Mrs. Leggett shook her hips and let out another shout. "Ha!"

Frank's eyes swept over the room and widened when they fell on me. His face turned red. "Mother," he groaned, reaching forward to turn off the music. "Please."

I glanced at Mrs. Greene. She held a hand up to her lips, clearly holding back a smile. I fought a grin of my own. "Here, Frank." I held up the chicken. "This is Mildred."

● ● ●

Frank switched on the light in the bomb shelter and looked around. "Gee, I don't know where to put her." He rubbed the back of his neck. "I suppose I could build a small attachment on the side to use as a coop. What does she eat? Corn?"

I shrugged. "Yeah, I guess so."

"Here, let me see her." Frank reached out and took the hen, cradling it in his arms. At first Mildred protested, ruffling her feathers, but under Frank's soothing hands, she soon settled down. "She's got a pretty coloring. Nice feathers, strong talons." Frank glanced at me accusatorily. "And you were going to eat her."

"Well, actually the shut-ins were going to eat her."

"Right." Frank gave me a lopsided grin and began settling hay in a corner of the shelter. His tanned hands smoothed out the rough bed before he set Mildred on top of it. "This'll have to do until I can build that coop." He frowned. "I hope she doesn't keep the other animals up at night."

"She won't. She's good, I know."

We stepped out as Frank closed the door behind us. Up on the hill, his house stood proud and bright. Mrs. Leggett and Mrs. Greene were visible in the big window. Mrs. Leggett obviously had the cha-cha music back on, because she was showing her guest how to shake her hips with great enthusiasm.

Frank groaned and leaned against the shed. "My mother is very embarrassing." He waved a hand at the window.

I shrugged. "Everyone has their peculiarities. My mom slathers lotion on *everything*. You can tell where she's been by the residue left on doorknobs." I chuckled and nudged him. "And you? You'll probably grow up to be the male equivalent of the eccentric cat lady." I began to laugh.

Frank laughed—that full, rumbling laugh that turned his face from a simple ray into the glowing sun. He shook his head at me. "And your house will be so confused with different baking smells that your children will constantly be grossed out."

"I suppose so." I slid against the shed and settled on the dirt, watching the women dancing from the window.

Frank settled beside me. "Has anyone ever told you that your laugh is infectious?"

My brow furrowed. "What do you mean?"

"When you laugh, it makes me want to laugh too. I don't know why, but it does."

"Huh." I drew my knees up to my chest. "Now that's something I never knew about myself. Cliff's never mentioned it. He talks a lot about my birthmark but never my laugh."

"Oh, you mean this?" Frank's hand brushed my cheek.

"Yeah." I touched the small indent in the corner of my mouth. A little larger than a dimple. A bit smaller than a scar. It was just a little dent. Hardly noticeable, really. At least, no one outside of my family had ever mentioned it to me. Until now.

"My mother would say that means you were kissed by an angel. When you were born, I mean."

"Really?" I smiled softly. My chest felt all tight and fluttery under his gaze. What could a boy like this possibly see in Juli?

"Yeah." He grinned back.

I lowered my eyes, wrapping a strand of hair around my finger.

"Scarlett!"

I looked up to see Mrs. Greene standing on the top of the hill. "Come on!" she shouted. "I told your mom I'd have you home by seven! It's almost eight!"

"Coming!" I stood and brushed off my jeans. "I guess I'll see you tomorrow."

Frank nodded. "Right. At the peach stand. Make sure Cliff's got his sign ready."

"I will. Okay, well, good-bye." I smiled and ran up the hill toward Mrs. Greene. *I can't wait until tomorrow.*

Chapter 7

You cannot be serious."

I tore my eyes away from the sign to glare at Cliff. He stood proudly in his freshly washed shirt and trousers, his hair slicked back with an unnecessary amount of gel. He gave me a smug smile and wrapped an arm around his sign. The smell of fresh paint still lingered in the air. "Don't you like it?"

"Cliff!" I threw up a hand, exasperated. "It's in Spanish!"

¡Pasteles de melocotón en venta!! the sign read, in sprawling blue letters. A large painting of a peach sat in the bottom corner, while a sun graced the top.

This is weird. Even for Cliff, this is really weird.

My head was beginning to hurt. I rubbed my forehead and prepared to turn on my heel. As I did so, I saw Cliff's brows had knotted.

"Is something wrong, Scarlett?"

I rolled my eyes. "How did you even know how to spell *peaches* in Spanish?"

He shrugged. "From the Spanish translation dictionary you gave me for Christmas."

Drat. He had begged me for that dictionary. Then he'd walked around the house spewing out Spanish words for weeks.

"There's only one solution." I stepped back and rubbed my neck.

"You're going to have to repaint it—and fast." I shot him a look. "In *English*."

Out of the corner of my eye, I watched Cliff paint as I arranged the pies on the stand. The warm, tangy peach scent tickled my nose. *Oh, they smell so good. And they look so nice.* I couldn't help but feel especially proud of the presentation. The crust was perfectly flaky, the peaches perfectly gooey. It had been worth staying up late to get them all made.

"Yum!" a deep voice grumbled. Dad sauntered out of the side door, wearing a large smile on his face. He wrapped an arm around me and took a big whiff. "Did you make an extra pie for your old man?"

"No, but if you'd like one, they're only two dollars apiece." I scrunched up my nose and beamed at him.

Dad rubbed his stomach and leaned in to kiss my cheek. "I personally know how good my Scarlett is at cooking, so I'm going to buy two."

He reached into the pockets of his faded jeans and pulled out a crumpled five-dollar bill. "I believe that will be four dollars and a tip. That makes …" He looked down and held up the bill. "Well, I believe that's five dollars exactly!"

Cliff whooped and snatched the money, doing a little victory dance. "Five dollars!"

Dad's eyes twinkled as he watched Cliff dance. Then he turned to me and winked before grabbing two pies and walking back up the driveway toward the house. The screen door slammed behind him.

"Hey, Cliff, how's that sign coming?"

Cliff held up the sign. *Peach Pies for Sale. Two dollars each.*

"Perfect." Stepping back, I looked over the table. *Once again, perfect.* "Okay, now all we have to do is wait."

The sun was hazy and warm overhead, making my head swarm.

The Georgia heat was intoxicating. I was grateful for the umbrella Frank had set up over the stand.

Cliff lay on his back in the grass and closed his eyes with a wide smile on his face. I itched to join him. *No, I'd better stay right here. A customer might come any minute.*

I looked down the dirt road. We were stationed at the end of the driveway, where it met the neighborhood road. Usually this road was pretty busy with folks going to church, the grocery store—anywhere, really. But today? Nothing. No cars, no bikes … Zip.

My eyes wandered back to the soft grass. Yes, soft. And warm and green and …

Okay, stop it. You never know when someone will show up. I wrapped a strand of hair around my finger. *Although … if a car came I would be able to hear it, wouldn't I?* And then I could jump up and be in my seat before they even got out.

"Knock, knock," Cliff said.

I sighed. *Really?* "Who's there?"

"Anita."

"Anita who?"

"Anita eat one of those pies. They smell real good, Scarlett."

I raised an eyebrow, pleased. "Well, I'm glad you like them, but we can't have any until we sell at least a few of them, okay?"

He frowned but didn't push the subject any further. We sat in silence for what felt like forever.

Finally, I inched out of the seat and onto the grass to sprawl out next to Cliff. I watched the bloated white clouds drift by. *Isn't it wild to think that this whole world is spinning—me along with it? It's sort of like flying.* The thought sent shivers of exhilaration all through me.

The sound of wheels on gravel jolted me out of my daydream. I sat up and saw Frank bicycling toward us with purpose. He skidded to a stop in front of the stand. "No customers?"

"Nope." I squinted up at him. His hair looked dazzlingly golden in the sunlight, although just yesterday I had thought it looked plain brown. *Funny*.

"Well, my mother sent me over with a request for three peach pies. We're having company tomorrow night."

I smiled but rolled my eyes. "Will they really need three whole pies?"

Frank shrugged. "Who knows? Hey, kid." He nudged Cliff with his foot, chuckling.

Cliff peeked at Frank with one eye. "Hey, I'm enjoying my *siesta*."

We were interrupted by the arrival of a car in the driveway. I jumped, feeling goose bumps pop up all over my arms. "A customer," I hissed, nudging Cliff with my own foot.

He sat up abruptly, and his entire body appeared to be on alert. "Who is it?"

"I don't know." I strained my eyes, trying to see into the window.

The baby blue car pulled to a stop, and the door popped open. Pastor Greene stuck his head out. "Good morning!"

His wife climbed out of the passenger side, her hair piled high upon her head. She waved. "How's business?"

I licked my lips nervously. "Well … you know." *Slow.*

Frank straightened and shook Pastor Greene's hand. "Good morning, sir."

Pastor Greene squinted and looked over the pies. "Some nice confections you've got here. My wife tells me you're a great cook. Did you have any trouble building the stand?"

Pastor Greene was wearing slacks and a white shirt with the sleeves rolled up. A straw hat was in his hand, politely held by his side. It felt so strange to see him without a suit and tie. I blinked, realizing I hadn't answered his question.

"Um, no, sir. None at all," Frank jumped in. "Cliff and I did most of the construction together."

Pastor Greene nodded, pressing his lips together. He looked impressed. "You've obviously got a gift for carpentry."

I glanced at the stand. I hadn't realized it, but it really was nice, like something a handyman dad would build.

"Can we have two pies, please?" Mrs. Greene pulled a five-dollar bill out of her pocketbook. "I'm going to bring one to Mrs. Nice. She can't get out of the house herself, you know."

My eyes flickered to the ground. "Right." I accepted the money and stuffed it in our savings jar, then handed Mrs. Greene a dollar from the change stash I'd created. *Nine dollars.*

Pastor Greene picked up the pies, balancing them in his two hands. "I think this is the most delicious load I've ever had the pleasure of carrying for you, dear." He winked at his wife.

She turned back to me. "Scarlett, I've really got to run, but I'll be back for more pies next week. I promise." She squeezed my hand, leaning close enough for me to smell her lemony-fresh perfume. Then she dropped my hand and scurried back to their car.

They pulled out of the driveway just as another car pulled in. Cliff glanced at me, raising his eyebrows. I smiled. *We'll have that rocket in no time.*

● ● ●

The sun was just beginning to set, turning the sky into a warm palette of roses and peaches. Frank sighed and stretched out on the grass, closing his eyes. "Ugh. I don't want to leave."

Cliff nudged him. "You've got to go. We'll see you tomorrow."

Frank opened one eye and glanced at me. "Did I ever tell you that you have an ornery little brother?"

"What does *ornery* mean?" Cliff sat up. "Scarlett, what does that word mean?"

I smiled. My fingers flipped through the money quickly, smoothing out the bills. "At times I find him rather cantankerous."

Cliff's mouth dropped into a small *O*. "I don't know any of these words!"

"Sometimes he does act in a juvenile manner."

Cliff frowned. "How do you even know all these words without looking in a dictionary?"

I reached out and closed his mouth, pinching his chin. "But I find him absolutely congenial."

He made a face and squirmed away. Right. I forgot about the no-touching thing. But he still managed a small smile. "I'm going inside."

We watched him leave in silence. Then Frank climbed to his feet. "Hey, how much did we make?"

I patted the money. "Eleven dollars. Plus the money from the three pies your mom ordered. So that makes seventeen."

His eyebrows rose. "Why, if we keep doing that well, we'll have that rocket by the end of summer! We only need about fifty or sixty bucks for all the wood and metal supplies."

"Well, that's the plan." I shut down the stand and grabbed the last two pies, while Frank grabbed the three for his mom. The sweet, tangy smell still tickled my nose. "And we have two extras. One for you"—I balanced a pie on top of Frank's already large load—"and one for us. Good night!"

He took a big whiff of the pie, his lips curling up in childish delight. "Yum. Four pies in one night. Someone's going to have a stomachache tomorrow."

I rolled my eyes as he placed his collection of baked goods in a box he'd lashed to his handlebars, then headed home.

● ● ●

"Hey, Mama! I still have one pie left!" The door slammed behind me. I brushed into the kitchen and placed the pie on the counter. "We can eat it after supper!" The supper Mama had promised to make, since I'd be busy with the pie stand all day.

Silence. Mama wasn't in the kitchen. The counters were caked in grease and flour, the oven was still on, and cracked eggshells lay on empty plates. "Mama?" *Why would she just stop in the middle?*

Voices drifted in from the living room. Mama and Dad.

I tiptoed through the hallway, a sick feeling in my stomach. My conscience was itching. *I don't have to sneak. This is my house. I can just walk in and—*

"No, Bill, you really don't understand." Mama's voice sounded tense. Stressed.

"It's just twenty bucks. I don't get how that's a problem."

"Of course you don't!" Mama sighed. "We just can't keep giving money to these different political groups. Our family has to have something to live off of too, you know. How do you expect me to buy groceries when our bread money is in some politician's bank account?"

I peeked through the crack of the living room door. Mama was sitting in the love seat, running a floured hand through her hair. She was still wearing an apron tied over her plantation outfit. Dad stood by the fireplace smoking a cigarette. He turned to her and stuck a hand in his pocket.

"Vida, we're making enough money. You've got your job at the bed and breakfast, and Mr. Leggett mentioned hiring me to do some extra work around the farm in August. You know we'll have enough to—"

"I don't know about my job," Mama hissed.

Dad halted, looking confused. "What do you mean?"

Mama's face darkened. She rubbed her cheekbones, brushing what remained of the flour onto her face. "The plantation house hasn't been doing very well. We've been getting very little business. The Cummins already had to let go of two workers in the last month." She lowered her voice and leaned against the mantle. "I'm just not sure how much longer they'll need me."

The room grew silent. I shivered in the ninety-degree heat and wrapped my arms around myself. I knew this was bad. What this could mean for our family. My stomach churned and, for a split second, I felt angry at both of them. Why couldn't they just work it out and kiss and make up like normal couples? Why did everything have to be so hard and complicated and secretive? It made me hate living there and having to act like I hadn't seen anything.

My cheeks flushed. *I shouldn't have thought that.* I didn't hate my life or anything about it. At least not that much.

Dad stepped forward and laid a hand on Mama's shoulder. She turned abruptly and bolted away from him, heading for the door. I jumped, feeling like a snoop. *Great.*

Without thinking, I began climbing the staircase. The living room door opened, and Mama stepped out. She glanced up. "Scarlett!" Her voice hesitated. "When did you get in?"

"Oh, hi!" I said brightly. *Just act natural. Just act natural. Maybe they didn't hear you earlier.* My lips pressed together, heat warming my cheeks. "I just came in. I'm going to go up and change out of these sticky clothes. I brought an extra pie if you want one." *I am the worst liar on earth.* It was probably written all over my face. "Um, I'll come down in a few minutes and finish up supper, okay?" I turned on my heel and practically ran up the rest of the stairs.

Supper was quiet, as usual, and without my sister. Cliff and Grandpop Barley decided to go to bed early, so there were also no Spanish Civil War narratives that night.

By the time I trudged upstairs and headed to my room, the sky was continuing to fade, the peachy pinks fading into a dusky purple. I switched on the lamp in my room and began to undress, pulling on my pajamas. I was just fastening the last button when the door opened suddenly and Juli walked in. She threw a bag onto the ground and nodded to me. "Hey."

I blinked. I knew I was supposed to say something friendly and encouraging, but the only thing that came to mind was, "Oh. You're home."

"Yeah, well …" Without stopping to take off her shoes, Juli collapsed onto her bed. "I'm pretty beat." Her words were muffled in the pillow.

I sat on the edge of my bed and looked her over. Her sandaled feet were dirty. Stains and smears covered her long skirt, and there were small cuts on her arms. Everything about her seemed skinny and dirty and weak.

My nose pinched at the smell of her clothes. Grass and sweat and something else I couldn't quite make out. "Did Mama and Dad see you, Juli?"

She groaned and rolled around until she lay on her back. "Nah. I came in the back door and hid in the kitchen until I heard Mama leave the living room. Dad stayed in there, and she went to her bedroom. They had another fight, I guess." Her cheeks puffed out. "Gosh, sometimes I really just hate being here."

The bitterness in her voice churned my stomach. I clutched a pillow, feeling guilty because I had been so close to thinking that only a few minutes earlier. "They didn't have a fight. They just had … a disagreement about some money." My voice didn't sound very confident. I gnawed on my bottom lip.

Juli rolled her eyes. "They wouldn't worry about money if Dad was less of a bum and actually went out to get a real job or something."

What? My skin turned hot. I sat up, tensing. "Don't you dare say that, Juli! Dad works just as hard as anyone. We all work together. All except for you. But I guess you wouldn't be home enough to know that anyway, would you?" The words that spilled out of my tongue were venomous and beyond repetition. I felt like spitting at Juli. *Stupid, selfish sister!*

Juli glared back, daring me with her flashing eyes. "I don't see why they don't just get rid of Grandpop Barley right now. The longer they put it off, the more the bills are going to stack up."

I stood, only inches away from her. It felt like she was trying to egg me on, waiting to see what I would do. I clenched my fists at my side. "Grandpop Barley is family! He's not going anywhere!"

"He's just an expensive freak. Like Cliff."

That straw broke the camel's back, and my hand flew of its own accord, slapping Juli clean across the cheek. Juli whipped right back, hitting me harder. It knocked the breath out of me and I stood there panting, staring at her. At my older sister. The one who played dolls with me and braided my hair and taught me how to whistle through my missing front teeth. My hand was throbbing. *Did I really just hit her?*

Juli's face grew very white. Then her mouth opened with a spew of curse words I'd never heard before. She grabbed her bag. "Ziggy's more family to me than you are." The door slammed behind her and then I was alone again.

I didn't hear her footsteps on the stairs or her car pull out of the driveway. It was just silent. Mama called upstairs, wanting to know what was wrong, but I just shouted, "Nothing!" and turned off the light.

Then I curled up on my bed and stared into the darkness, wondering when I had turned into the kind of girl who thought bad things about her parents and slapped her sister in the face.

● ● ●

The house was perfectly quiet when I awoke close to midnight. Silently, I pushed back the covers and climbed out of bed. My throat burned from thirst.

I crept down the stairs and into the kitchen. Pulling a glass down from the cupboard, I filled it with water and gulped it down.

Pit. Pat.

I blinked. *What was that?*

Pat. Pit. Pit. There it was again: a strange tapping noise, coming from outside.

My heart began to race. Maybe someone was trying to break in. Maybe it was a notorious axe murderer who'd come to prey upon our family. Maybe ...

I hugged my chest. Well, there was only one way to find out. And someone would be screaming for help if it was a murderer, right?

It was probably only Juli, now that I thought about it. Mama probably locked the front door, and she needed me to come open it for her. Perhaps it was nothing.

I inched toward the side door. With trembling fingers, I pushed aside the curtain and peered through the little window. Utter darkness. *No, wait ...* I looked a little closer.

Someone was standing outside by the side of the house. A man, by the looks of it. His arm was raised, and he tossed something at the house. *Pit. Pat.* Rocks. He was throwing rocks at a window.

What on earth ...

I squinted my eyes as hard as I could. He looked an awful lot like ...

I unlocked the door and pulled it open slowly. "Frank?"

The man's head whipped toward me. Then he stepped forward into the moonlight. It was indeed Frank, standing in my front yard with a lightweight jacket thrown over his pajamas. "Oh, hey, Scarlett."

I pushed the door open all the way and stepped out into the

yard, still holding my arms tightly across my chest. I shook my head. "What are you doing here? In the middle of the night?"

"Oh, actually, I was trying to throw rocks at Cliff's window. I found the most amazing thing, and I really wanted him to see it."

A smile twitched in the corner of my lips. I pointed at the window he was standing in front of. "And so you threw rocks at that window?"

Frank glanced at the window and rubbed his forehead. "Well, yeah. I figured Cliff would wake up and then he could come out for just a while."

I cleared my throat, trying not to laugh. "Frank, you were throwing rocks at my parents' window. That's their bedroom. Cliff's is over to the left."

Frank's eyes grew large. "Oh." He paused. "I guess that would have been somewhat problematic."

I laughed, leaning against the door. "So what is it you wanted to show Cliff?"

He smiled. "It's a secret. For both of you."

Both of us? My stomach jumped, but I cleared my throat and tried to look serious. "You know you really are annoying? I mean, it's twelve o'clock at night."

"Twelve o'clock in the morning," Frank corrected, sticking his hands behind his back. "If it's a.m., then you say it's in the morning."

"I know that. Obviously." I looked him over. The whole thing was just really ridiculous. Frank, flinging rocks at my parents' window? Me and Cliff, sneaking out at midnight to go for a walk in the woods? Running around outside in our pajamas? I pressed my lips together, holding back a smile. "You stay right here. I'll go wake up Cliff."

Chapter 8

A re your eyes still closed?"

I sighed. "Yes."

"Okay. No peeking now."

Frank's hand was pressed firmly over mine, leading me through the woods. "Tree ahead," he warned, pulling me out of the way.

Cliff clutched my other arm. "You know, it's kind of scary to be in the woods in the dark. I've never been outside in the middle of the night."

Me either.

Frank halted to a stop, nearly causing me to run into him. "Okay. Now open your eyes."

My eyes flew open. Instantly, the beauty overwhelmed me. We stood in the middle of a moonlight-bathed clearing in the woods. The starry heavens reflected off a small, shallow pond. Rocks lay scattered on the forest floor.

I perched on a rock and hugged my knees to my chest. My thin sweater still let in a nip of the nighttime breeze, which tickled my neck and lifted the hairs on my forehead. "Wow. It's magical."

"Yeah, but this is what I really wanted to show you. Look." Frank knelt by the pond and turned on his flashlight. Swimming around in the shallow water were dozens of inky little tadpoles. Their tales swished around, and they darted under the cover of the pond's pebbles, startled by the sudden light.

"Whoa." Cliff lay on his stomach, watching the creatures in awe. "They're baby frogs, right?"

"Right." Frank switched off his flashlight. "But they don't like the harsh light. Besides, it's more fun to watch them swim in the dark anyway."

We watched them in silence for a long time—all of us spread out on our stomachs. The way they sporadically darted back and forth, into the murky shadows and then back into the moonlight, was mesmerizing.

My head began to swim in circles too, bewitched by the moonlight and sweet evening scent. The woods felt heavy and peaceful around us. The whole world lay still.

"Hey," Frank whispered after a while. "I think he fell asleep." He nodded at Cliff, who was lying beside me with his face buried in his arms.

I nudged him with my elbow. "Cliff?"

He didn't move; his breathing grew heavier.

Frank made a face. "Ah, let him sleep. I'll carry him home later."

My fingers messed with the little curls on Cliff's neck just above his pajama collar. He would have slapped my hand away if he had been awake, but there are zero no-touching rules when you're sound asleep. "He's probably really tired." I glanced up. "After all, it is twelve o'clock *in the morning*."

"Mmm." Frank watched him in silence for several seconds. I wanted to know what he was thinking, but I was afraid to ask.

Instead, I rolled up my sleeves and pressed my elbows into the cool dirt. With one finger, I drew a tic-tac-toe board in the soil. I glanced up at Frank. "You go first."

He grinned, and drew a big *O* in the right corner.

I frowned. "You know you're supposed to start every game in the middle square. It's the best guarantee of winning."

He shrugged. "I've won this way before."

Okay. I rolled my eyes and drew an *X* in the center.

Frank whistled softly as he contemplated his next move. "Would you rather be rich or be famous?"

A smile crept across my face. "Neither. I'd rather be smart."

He made a face and drew another *O* in the dirt. "That wasn't an option."

"Still. It was better than either of the alternatives." I rested my chin in my cupped hands. "Would you rather be an astronaut or a doctor?"

"Um, a doctor." He held up a hand. "But only a pet doctor. A veterinarian."

"Oh, right." I squished the cool dirt between my fingers, letting it cake under my nails. I could see Frank as a veterinarian. Actually, that sounded really great. He could do what he loved every day of his life—rescuing animals and taking care of them. And he would get paid for it.

Frank squinted at me in the darkness. "Would you rather be a character in a book or a movie?"

"Movie. But only if it's a major hit and I could be played by a famous person." Not that I really knew of that many famous people. But still.

He nodded. "Same."

I pressed my lips together. The forest around us was quiet and still; the three of us seemed to be the only ones in the world.

I thought about Mrs. Greene and the chicken incident. About her talking about her life and how she met her husband, and how when he read to her, she knew what he was saying was true. I wondered if I would ever know anything to be true like that.

Frank was watching me and waiting. *Oh, my turn.* "Sorry," I muttered, marking an *X*.

"What are you thinking?" he asked softly.

I sighed. "Would you rather die and not know where you're going or live forever on earth with no hope of going anywhere at all?"

A frown crossed his face. He cleared his throat. "I'd never really thought about it. I guess when you're eighteen it feels like you'll be living forever anyway. Like it'll be ages until you have to start worrying about that."

"Yeah, I guess." My head hurt just thinking about it. The world beyond ours seemed big and scary. *If astronauts can't see the end of it, just how big would a God and a heaven beyond it be?*

Frank chuckled and drew his last *O*. "Three in a row. What did I tell you?"

I jolted to attention. Sure enough, three *O*s. I grinned sheepishly. "I just wasn't paying attention."

"Says the loser."

He stared at the ground for a while, a self-satisfied smirk on his face. Then he glanced up at me. "Can I ask you … I know this probably isn't …" He took a quick breath and lowered his voice. "Is there something wrong with Cliff? I mean, everyone says he's … Well, they say he's crazy, and he certainly acts like no one else I know. I was just wondering …" A crease formed on his forehead. "I mean, have you taken him to any doctors or anything? To figure out what the problem is?"

I dropped my eyes. *Why does everyone always seem to think he has a problem?* Emotions flooded through me. Red-hot anger at someone thinking my brother was crazy, ice-cold sadness at the fact that people always recognized he was different and that was all that seemed to matter to them, and several other feelings that I couldn't name. Confusion, I guess. And embarrassment.

The silence slowly built around us. I realized with a jolt that I hadn't answered Frank's question. I peeked up at him and opened my mouth to speak, but stopped when I saw his face, twisted in what looked like regret. He glanced down as my eyes met his and messed with the laces on his shoes. "I'm sorry, I shouldn't have—"

I shook my head to stop him. "It's okay." I shrugged, folding my arms across my chest. "I don't know what's wrong with Cliff. We've never talked to any doctors. I guess Dad and Mama have always just kind of hoped he'd grow out of it. But he's ten now, so I guess he won't."

Frank looked away. I exhaled, releasing all the tension in my body. The air felt welcoming and cool again. I tapped my fingers on my arms, looking down at Cliff's sleeping head close by my knees. "The only thing I know for sure about Cliff is that he's the most amazing and special person I know."

Frank smiled softly. "I think you and Cliff are both very special." He dipped his finger into the pond, drawing little circles in the water. "That's why ..." He paused. "That's why I asked you both to come here tonight." He looked up at me. "I've never shown this little pond to anyone before. I just like to come out here to be alone sometimes and to sit and think." Another pause. "But tonight, when I came out here, it was all quiet and still and all the baby tadpoles were darting around and I couldn't help but wish ..." His voice grew husky. "Well, I suddenly wanted you both to be here too. I guess that seems silly."

My eyes lowered. "I don't think it seems silly at all." It seemed nice. Really nice, actually. He was quiet again. I was quiet as well, and I could feel the silence stretching around us, wrapping us up into this big blanket of something that felt thick and tangible and *real*.

Maybe that's what our friendship was. It was the feeling that we didn't have to speak or explain. We could sit in the darkness and watch the tadpoles just as easily as we could lie out in the heat and breathe in the smell of peaches and gravel, all without saying a word.

I ran my fingertips through the cool water. The reflection of the crescent moon quivered on the surface of the pond.

"And look at this moonlight." Frank smirked. "You look absolutely smashing, Scarlett."

I laughed and inched myself closer to the water. "Dad has a Bing Crosby record I listen to sometimes. It has a song called 'Moonlight Becomes You.' Juli thinks it's silly, but I've always believed that everything looks better by the light of the moon. Don't you think?"

A crisp evening breeze fluttered the tips of my hair. I wrapped a curl around my finger and began to sing softly. "Moonlight becomes you; it goes with your hair. You certainly know the right thing to wear. Moonlight becomes you, I'm thrilled at the sight. And I could get so romantic tonight ..." I trailed off, my face heating. *Of all the ways to appear immature and childish, singing an old-fashioned song in a midnight grove is probably at the top of the list.* I cleared my throat. "I guess I have a sentimental attachment to old music. It's just so much softer and happier, don't you think?"

Frank didn't answer. He was staring at my hair. It was loose and, I hoped, still falling around my shoulders in tousled waves.

Self-consciously, I brushed it out of my face. "I know, I know. I have really messy hair." A half smile pulled at my lips.

He met my eyes with a grin. "You must have been a really cute kid, Scarlett." His face suddenly grew serious, his eyes big and solemn. "Can I ask you one more question?"

"Shoot." I tried to keep my smile loose, although I suddenly felt pinned under his stare.

Frank's face turned serious. "This may sound kind of mean, but why don't you have friends?" Seeing me tense, he leaned forward and grabbed my hand. "Oh, I'm sorry. I didn't mean it like ... I just ... you and Cliff are just so great, but no one seems to ever, you know, talk to you or anything. Why doesn't everyone want to be close to you all the time? If they took the time ..." He trailed off, and I was subconsciously aware that he was still holding my hand, even though he seemed to have forgotten about it. "I know you had some problems with Cliff when he was little. Is that it?"

I took a deep breath and shook my head slowly. "Cliff's always been kind of strange. You remember that time in church when he was six and he stood up and recited the Pledge of Allegiance in the middle of the pastor's prayer?"

Frank nodded, a smile growing on his face. I figured he'd remember that. It was kind of an infamous story.

"Everyone stared at him and started whispering. I wanted to ... . . " I bit back my words; I remembered the hot anger that had boiled beneath my skin that day. "The next day at school, I punched Billy Winters in the face for calling Cliff an idiot. I got sent home with a warning from my teacher, and the next day when I came back, all the kids in my class were giving me the silent treatment. Turns out Billy's little girlfriend, Amanda Berkley, had told all the girls that I was a freak and me and my brother were contaminated with germs." I ran a hand over the ground and dug in my finger-nails. "So I didn't talk to them anymore, and they didn't talk to me. Well, to either of us. Cliff and I did our classes separately and then sat together at lunch, recess, and the bus ride. We avoided everyone, and everyone acted like we didn't exist."

"Oh." Frank breathed the word; it escaped from his lips like a half-silent sigh. "I do sort of remember that now that you mention it. But I was never avoiding you—on purpose, at least. I was just never brave enough to talk to you, or to Cliff. Besides, I was older, so there was this whole thing about not talking to younger kids or risking ..." He lowered his gaze. "You know how it is in grade school."

I did know how it was in grade school. I don't know why I expected him to say anything differently or come up with some good excuse as to why he had avoided me. It's not like it mattered now. "It's okay." I felt my chest deflate though. "I know how it is. That's life." I forced a fake smile.

Frank looked up and met my eyes. "No," he said. "It was wrong of me. If I could go back, I would have talked to you that day when you punched Billy Winters. I would have talked to you every day for the past four years. I would have …" He trailed off, watching me. I could see the golden specks in his green eyes, half hidden under his thick eyelashes.

For a full three seconds, time froze. The air seemed to vibrate, humming some tune that I couldn't quite hear. Every hair felt like it was standing up on edge under his gaze.

And then Frank climbed to his feet and brushed off his pants, and the moment was broken. The night was silent, except for the sound of crickets, and my heart had gone back to a relatively normal beat.

"Come on," Frank muttered, lifting Cliff in his arms. He glanced at me. "It's a good thing your brother's so skinny." He nodded for me to follow him and began heading back to the house.

I looked over my shoulder for one last glance of the soft moonlight filtered through the trees. Immature or not, I couldn't help thinking that there never was a more beautiful night.

• • •

Car headlights blinded us as we walked up the driveway. For an instant, I froze, my heart beating. *Have Mama and Dad been looking for us? Were they worried?*

Juli hopped out of her car. An oversized jacket was wrapped around her thin shoulders. Probably Ziggy's.

She looked the three of us over: me huddled in my sweater and pajamas, Cliff sound asleep, and Frank hauling him in his arms.

Frank reddened. "Hi, Juli." His voice sounded hoarse.

"Hello."

I doubted Juli knew Frank's name, or even who he was. Even though he'd probably been in all of her classes since sixth grade. She knew absolutely nothing about him other than the fact he was standing on our doorstep at one in the morning with Cliff in his arms. Which probably didn't impress her much, given her recent appraisal of our little brother.

"Um ... So what have you been doing?" Frank stammered. With his free hand, he reached up to push the hair off his forehead.

Juli shrugged. "Not much." She glanced at me out of the corner of her eyes as she shut her car door. "In fact, I've been in my room all evening, haven't I, Scarlett? Sleeping all night." She grinned. "Just like you have."

My stomach churned. *Blackmail, seriously?* Juli was forcing me into lying about her whereabouts by threatening to tell *mine*?

I mumbled something like "Yeah, sure," and motioned for Frank to put Cliff down. I wrapped my arm around Cliff's shoulder. "I think I've got him now." My eyes flickered up and caught Frank's. "Thanks for coming. I had fun."

"Yeah, me too." He stuck his hands in his pockets and turned to leave.

"Oh, wait." Juli's voice startled us both. She wrapped her arms around herself and glanced at Frank. "Do you know anything about cars? Because my engine was making a weird sound, and I don't really want the parents to know that I was driving it tonight." She raised her eyebrows. "I just don't think they'd be real understanding, you know?"

"Oh yeah, right." Frank's face was a whole new shade of red. He was shaking, probably with excitement over the prospect of getting to help the all-great-and-wonderful Juli with her car problems.

I made a face, unnoticed, and began dragging Cliff upstairs. I tucked him back into his bed and shut the door. My bedroom was empty. *Juli must still be outside with Frank.*

The blinds were wide open, letting in the moonlight. I crossed to the window and peered into the darkness.

Juli and Frank were standing by the car. Frank had his flashlight turned on and was looking under the hood. He laughed about something and shook his head before closing the hood and unrolling his sleeves. Juli looked embarrassed. She laughed too and ran a hand through her long hair. She gave Frank a little wave before disappearing inside. Frank stood staring after her for several seconds, flashlight in hand, before he turned and left.

The bedroom door opened a few minutes later, and Juli entered. "After all that, there was just something stuck under the hood." She chuckled.

"Huh." I pulled off my sweater and crawled back into bed. I didn't want to look at Juli or listen to her stupid car problems. *What did she say that made Frank laugh?*

Juli slipped out of her long dress and pulled on an old nightgown. She didn't seem intoxicated or distant. Traces of the old Juli were present in her smirking face, laughing at her own stupidity. "What was that guy's name?"

"Frank," I muttered into the sheets.

"Hmm." Juli seemed to think this over. "He seemed ... sweet. Good-looking too." She bit her lip, pausing over her bed. "Have I met him before? His face seemed familiar, but I wasn't really sure."

I rolled my eyes. "You've been going to school with him since you were ten."

"Really?" Juli's eyebrows shot up. "Yeah, I thought I recognized him," she said, climbing into bed and tucking the covers around herself. "Well, I guess he's one thing to look forward to this summer. Can't think of much else." With that, she rolled over and fell silent.

I stared at the ceiling, imagining the swirling tadpoles and Cliff's sleepy little curls and the look on Frank's face when he said I must have been a cute kid.

• • •

"Scarlett?"

Without raising my head, I called back, "In the kitchen!" My hands flew as I diced the celery and carrots. *Chicken pot pie. Yum.*

Mama stuck her head in the doorway. "Grandpop Barley's acting kind of strange. Do you think you could take him for a walk or something? Your father and I are going to a political meeting, and I have to get my hair ready."

How can Grandpop Barley be acting "strange"? The very definition of Grandpop Barley is "strange." Though I'd noticed he'd been especially prickly all day—and he didn't have the excuse of getting too little sleep last night.

I wrinkled my nose. "Take him for a walk? He's not a dog."

Mama groaned. "Please, Scarlett." Her long fingernails tapped on the doorway.

I looked down at the chopped vegetables in front of me. "What about supper?"

"I'll finish it after I set my hair. It just has to go in the oven, right? Piece of cake."

Chicken pot pie, actually, and it's not even put together yet. It was no use fighting with Mama though. She had the will of a team of oxen, Dad often said.

"Fine." I set down the knife and pulled off my apron. "Where is he?"

"Upstairs getting dressed. Your dad and I are leaving in thirty minutes. Come back when the pie is ready, and you three can eat. Heaven knows where Juli is." Mama disappeared, leaving the residue of her lotioned hands on the door frame.

I climbed the stairs slowly, wondering where I was going to take Grandpop Barley. The only thing he hated more than baths was people, and people were everywhere these days. Sitting on their porches, playing in their yards, standing by their mailboxes … There was no way to avoid them.

Grandpop was standing at the top of the stairs, waiting for me with a hat jammed onto his head. He cleared his throat and crossed his arms. "Well, have you come to take me or not?" he asked in a gruff voice.

I tried not to wince. *That red tie.* It was streaked with chocolate and peanut butter and who knows what else. And yet it remained stubbornly tied around his wrinkled neck like a sailor's knot. Or a hangman's noose.

"Yep. Are you ready?"

Grandpop Barley frowned. "Let me grab my sweater."

I stood in the doorway and looked over his shoulder as he grabbed a faded gray cardigan. "It's eighty degrees outside."

"So?" His brow furrowed. "I've known people to catch cold in that kind of weather! I'm too old to catch a cold. It'll be the death of me!"

"Okay, okay, calm down." I helped him pull on the sweater and fasten the little brass buttons. *I'm more concerned about overheating at the moment.* "Let's grab Cliff and go."

● ● ●

People stared at us while we walked by. Their watching eyes followed us, accompanied by whispers and stifled giggles.

My skin bristled. I was aware of the public opinion of Grandpop Barley and Cliff, but I didn't agree with it. Granted, they were both a little odd, but was that really such a big deal? Was it really so strange to see a seventy-year-old man hobbling along with an eagle-topped cane and a peanut butter–smeared tie alongside a little boy clutching a Spanish soldier figurine and rambling on about Hemingway?

I puffed out my cheeks and sighed. Oh, why deny it? Goodness gracious, we were a walking weirdo parade. And I was the ringleader.

Grandpop Barley halted to a stop in the middle of the street. *Garumph.* I nearly collided into the back of him. I frowned and reached forward to grab his wrist. "Come on, before a car comes or something."

He shook his head and pointed to the mailbox that read *Mrs. Ima Nice.* I stifled a moan. What did he want with Mrs. Nice?

"Ima was an old friend of mine." A thread of longing appeared in his voice. "Do you think we could …"

"George?" A raspy voice called. "George Barley?"

My head shot up. Mrs. Nice was sitting on the porch, squinting at us. She brightened when we turned, smiling at Grandpop Barley. "Why, it's me! Ima Kilpatrick."

"Ima!" A faint smile appeared on Grandpop Barley's face. He pulled off his hat and held it to his chest, his eyes glowing. Every senile, peanut-buttery, crotchety old part of him seemed to disappear. Grandpop Barley temporarily lost his Grandpop-Barley-ness. Instead, he just looked like a regular man standing at the edge of the driveway and smiling up at Mrs. Nice. "I haven't seen you in years."

Cliff glanced at me, bewildered. I shrugged, unsure what to make of the situation. How do you explain insanely sudden sanity?

But Grandpop Barley obviously intended on seeing Ima Nice. He began hobbling toward the house with a quickened step. "Well, how are you? How are you doing?"

Mrs. Nice smoothed down the hair around her gray bun and folded her hands in her lap. "Please sit."

Grandpop Barley settled in one of the empty rocking chairs,

clutching his hat. His eyes caressed Mrs. Nice with startling fondness. "How have you been, Ima?"

Her face blushed a youthful shade of pink. "Oh, I've been getting along okay. I've been raising chickens." She nodded at us. "Your grandkids come over for egg collection every Tuesday morning. Well, almost every Tuesday." She shot me a look.

"After eight," Cliff piped up.

Grandpop Barley nodded. "Yes, I've had some of the eggs. They were very good."

As if you could taste them smothered in peanut butter. I wrinkled my nose.

The sound of the creaking rockers filled the porch. The air was sticky and sweet, enveloping us in silence.

Mrs. Nice and Grandpop Barley smiled at each other like schoolchildren, glancing down bashfully every few seconds. Cliff and I also eyed each other. We sat on the steps, watching them in confusion. Cliff, who didn't seem to understand people all that well, was making faces and acting irritated. I didn't blame him. At the moment, I was starting to question what I knew about people too.

"Well," Grandpop Barley said after a while. "We'd better get home. We're having supper soon."

"Oh." Mrs. Nice's voice sounded resigned. She reached out and touched him with a leathery, pale hand, squeezing his arm. "Well, it was a pleasure to see you again, George."

"You too." Grandpop Barley's eyes softened. Then he stood and lifted his hat to his brow.

I scurried to my feet, pulling Cliff up with me. "Good to see you, Mrs. Nice." I nodded my head respectfully. Cliff bounded down the steps.

Grandpop Barley looked over his shoulder as he walked down the driveway, smiling to himself. "Fine woman," he murmured, fingering his moustache.

I glanced at him. "Did you know her when you were younger? Were you friends or sweethearts or something?"

He didn't answer me, likely lost again in his own little world of peanut butter and neckties. But his step was lighter, and his face softer for the rest of the day.

● ● ●

I lay very still on my bed and stared unblinkingly at the ceiling. It was early morning, and everything always felt really nice in the early morning. You kind of forgot whatever you were mad about the day before, and you were only concerned about all the wonderful things that could happen that day. At least that's how it always seemed to me.

Millions of thoughts rushed through my mind—some happy, some sad, some fearful. But also hopeful ones, like the kind you have when the rain is almost over and the sun is peeking out.

Something told me the sun was going to be peeking out soon on my family. Even after weeks of rain, the sun can't stay away forever.

The bedroom door opened, and Juli stuck her head in. "Hey." She closed the door behind her and threw her bag onto the bed. She smiled, a rare thing. "What are you up to?"

I squinted at her, vaguely suspicious. "Just thinking." *Was she out all night? Did she just get back, or has she been here for hours and woke up before me?*

"Huh." Juli kicked back and rested her head on her pillow. She stared up at the ceiling too, with the same thoughtful expression. It struck me that we were still sometimes alike.

I rolled over onto my stomach so I could see her. "You know, sometimes I just lie around and think through all the things I'm unsure of. Like whether love is real or imaginary. Whether chickens can tell what you're saying. Whether or not you can fall in love at first sight or know that there's a God or heaven or someone out there for you somewhere." I smirked. "Just your basic teenage thoughts."

Juli pursed her lips. "I think there's a divine happiness out there that brings about peace to the opened mind."

I blinked. "Oh." *Where did that come from? And what does it even mean? Is that Juli's way of trying to be mature and progressive, or does she actually believe that?* My mind felt strained, trying to understand the meaning of "divine happiness." It didn't sound like anything I'd ever heard in church. But then again, Juli didn't exactly have a Sunday-morning kind of philosophy on life.

Juli rolled over onto her stomach as well and propped herself up with her elbows. "Ziggy knows lots of smart things like that. He talks about finding our inner self and becoming enlightened. You should try talking to him sometime. I bet you'd be really impressed."

I thought about Ziggy with his long blond hair and thick dark eyebrows, and who always smelled like gasoline and beer. A shudder ran through me. "That's okay."

An injured look flashed across Juli's face, and I remembered that she thought he was more like family to her than we were these days. "Ziggy's a great guy. All of you are just too closed-minded to give him a chance." She rolled her eyes and turned her back to me, curling into a ball.

I stared at her back for several more seconds before looking back at the ceiling in silence.

Divine happiness. Inner peace. Enlightenment. I rolled my eyes. *What a bunch of hippie talk.*

Chapter 9

I knocked on Mrs. Greene's door with a firm hand the second time I visited her. She opened the door and smiled. "How lovely of you to drop by, Scarlett," she joked.

Johnny Cash was playing in the background, his deep, trembling voice filling the house. She must have remembered what I said about Juli and Johnny Cash. That felt thoughtful and sweet in a way. I grabbed an apron from the kitchen and tied it around my waist.

Mrs. Greene was wearing a pale blue shift dress that matched her eyes. A sparkling rhinestone pin glistened in her hair. It was probably too dressy for everyday wear, but I didn't get the impression she cared. "I was thinking about making sweet potato casserole today. And maybe pork chops. What do you think?"

I nodded. "What about dessert?"

"Oh, I don't know." She blew a strand of hair off her forehead. "Banana cream pie?"

I raised my eyebrows. *Basic, but it will work.* "Sure, I guess." I set to work peeling sweet potatoes, and soon thin shavings floated toward the counter. At least until the metal knife nicked my hand. *Ouch.* I sucked my finger before holding it out. *No blood.*

Mrs. Greene glanced at me. "So what is your family doing for Independence Day, Scarlett?"

I shrugged. "When is it? Next Friday? I'm not really sure."

"Well, if you were interested, we're hosting a celebration in our backyard, down by the creek. There's going to be fried chicken and fireworks and baseball."

"Sounds fun." I finished peeling the last sweet potato and set it on the counter. "I'll tell Mama."

Mrs. Greene scooped the sweet potatoes into her apron and carried them across the kitchen to the cutting board. A flash of metal caught my eye as she pulled out the big knife and began to chop. "I was going to tell you about it anyway. I was hoping to enlist your services. You see, we're expecting about twenty people or so, and I just can't think of anything to make for dessert. Do you think you could make me three peach pies? I'd pay you for them, of course."

My back straightened. *Three peach pies! That's six dollars!* "Sure! I'd love to ... I mean, I'll talk to Cliff but I'm sure we ... Oh, and won't Frank be ..." The words jumbled in my mouth. I pressed my lips together and smiled. *And this wouldn't even be a Saturday.* "Yes. Definitely. We'll go to the orchard to pick up more peaches."

Mrs. Greene chuckled. "Good."

"Um." I tucked a strand of hair behind my ear. "I don't mean to pry, but I was just wondering ..." I cleared my throat. "Are the Leggetts invited to the party?"

A smile tugged at Mrs. Greene's cherry-red lips. "As long as they don't bring Mildred along in the form of fried chicken." She wiped her hands on her apron and began digging in a drawer. Her voice was hard to hear over the banging of pots and pans. "Have you seen my little chicken lately, Scarlett?"

"I saw her Tuesday. She looked very good, but she was a bit cranky at Frank for forgetting to put out her corn before he left." I made a face. "I don't know how he remembers what to feed each animal at five every morning. I don't think I'd remember which foot to put in which shoe on at that hour."

"You like him, don't you?"

My eyes shot up, shock flooding my body. "Of course I like him. He's sacrificed a lot for me and Cliff. I'm very grateful to him."

Mrs. Greene pulled out a large white pan. "Here it is. The perfect size for sweet potato casserole." She placed in on the counter and bit her lip. "Scarlett, look in that cabinet over there and see if you can find a medium-sized frying pan for the pork chops."

"Yes, ma'am." I knelt on the floor and opened the cabinet. Rows of silver pans were piled on top of each other. *Great.* I began pulling out giant frying pans and tiny baking dishes, searching for the perfect size.

"You know, sixteen is a funny age. I fell in love when I was sixteen, remember?"

I nodded. "After being sick." *Aha.* I pulled out a six-inch frying pan and held it up proudly then pulled myself to my feet.

Mrs. Greene glanced at me and went back to chopping. "I just want to make sure you're perfectly aware of …" She sighed. "Remember to distance yourself from getting too attached to any boy that isn't serious about you. When you're only sixteen years old, you still have so much growing up to do."

"Mrs. Greene." I turned and shot her my best *I have no idea what you're talking about* look. "Frank is my friend. Nothing more." The cabinet door shut with a bang at my feet. "Besides, Frank is in love with Juli."

She nodded and looked away. "I'm sorry. I know I'm not your mother. And I'm not sixteen either." She tapped her lip thoughtfully, looking out the window. Soft light filtered through the lacy curtains, making her face glow. "It was an interesting season in life. You're not a child; you're not a woman. You're just sort of stuck." She glanced at me. "You know what I mean?"

Unsure about what she wanted me to say, I just shrugged.

Mrs. Greene seemed satisfied enough with my noncommittal answer. She looked down at her recipe then pulled out a mixing bowl and grabbed some brown sugar, flour, and butter—ingredients for the casserole topping. "Have you ever read *Peter Pan*?"

I shook my head. "I don't read much. Cliff likes to hear *For Whom the Bell Tolls*, but I've got to say, after the third reading, I got pretty sick of it."

"Well, I've got a copy of *Peter and Wendy*, if you'd like to borrow it. It's my absolute favorite book." Mrs. Greene stared at the recipe again for a second. "Read it to Cliff. He'd enjoy it."

I hesitated. I hated reading, hated books, and hated reading books. But I hated *For Whom the Bell Tolls* more. *If she says Cliff would like it, I'm sure he would.* "Is it Spanish?"

"Nope. It takes place in London."

That sealed the deal. *Maybe Cliff will become interested in England, and I can read him books in normal English.* "Okay, I'll borrow it."

"Good." She turned back toward the oven, and I looked to see if she had pecans I could add to make the topping even better.

As I looked through the pantry, a question I'd had lingering in my mind tugged at me. *Ask her. Just do it. She won't think you're dumb.*

"Mrs. Greene ..." I hesitated, then spit it out. "What do you know about divine happiness?"

A frown creased her forehead. "I don't think I know anything about it. What do you mean by 'divine happiness'?"

I grabbed a jar of pecans then sat on one of her barstools, folding my arms on the counter. "Juli says that there's a spiritual force out there that brings peace to you, if you keep your mind open."

"Huh." Mrs. Greene sat across from me and tapped a finger on her chin. "Well, then maybe I do know something about divine happiness, but in a slightly different way."

She handed me the butter and motioned toward the stove. I grabbed a small pan and began melting the stick down.

"You see, Scarlett, I believe there is only one way to divine happiness, and that is through peace with God. But this peace cannot be made through keeping an open mind or even trying to live in peace and harmony." Her mouth twisted in a thoughtful frown. "The way mankind was created, the way he operates, is always going to be unpeaceful. No matter how much he seeks peace, he'll never find it on his own."

I cut in. "I don't understand. If someone wants peace and calm, why can't he have it?"

Mrs. Greene frowned and glanced at me. She set down the sweet potatoes and got very still. "What is it you want, Scarlett?"

My shoulders slumped. "I want *peace*. Peace from bickering and arguments and stress." I took a breath. It was awkward to talk about. I couldn't imagine Mrs. Greene knew anything about what we went through, day in and day out. With Grandpop Barley and Cliff and Juli and all the money problems. My voice was quiet. "I want to be able to be a family again."

"I see." Mrs. Greene put down her knife and looked at me. "Then I'm afraid I can't help you. The answer to the divine peace you're looking for won't solve all your problems or make things more peaceful in your family."

Something hot flashed in my chest. "Then why search for it at all? Why do people look for God if he can't help us at all?"

She shook her head, and her eyes softened. "I don't think you understand what I'm trying to tell you, Scarlett. I never said God wouldn't help you at all. I just said he wouldn't help you in the way you want. The beauty of salvation and God's grace isn't in him solving all of our problems instantly, like a magic genie. Its beauty comes in the assurance that he has a greater plan for you."

I calmed the questions bubbling up in my throat and tried to listen to her as I began mixing the topping together. My head felt thick trying to process the information.

"When I was sixteen, I realized I needed God, not to get rid of

the turmoil in my life, but to eliminate the turmoil in my heart."
She rested a hand on her chest. "Because the real problem was me.
The problem was that no matter how hard I tried to do right, I did
wrong. I couldn't make myself good. It was a feeling of complete
hopelessness."

Her words tugged at my heart. I bit my lip. "So what did you do?"

"Well, the more Tim read to me from the Bible, I realized there
was a way out. I ..." She paused, a tremor in her voice. "I realized
that there was nothing I could do but trust in Christ. And it has
brought me such peace, Scarlett. Not the absence of trouble or heart-
ache, but the strength to endure it. And the assurance that nothing
will take him away from me. It's amazing, really."

"Huh." I stared at my hands on the counter. It sounded so good.
But Juli's words had sounded good too. How was I supposed to
know which was right and which was wrong?

I can't deal with this right now. I pushed away from the counter
and forced a bright smile on my face. "Well, let's get this casserole
put together and in the oven. We've got lots of meals to fix!"

● ● ●

"Does it have any Spanish in it?"

I glanced at the book and shook my head. "No," I said dryly.

Cliff raised an eyebrow. "Any spaceships? Any astronauts?"

"Any peanut butter?" Grandpop Barley called from the armchair
in Cliff's room. Since my parents were off at another political thing,
I kind of had to keep him close by.

A smile threatened to escape my tightly pressed lips. "I don't
think so. Now do you two want to hear it or not?"

Cliff shrugged and snuggled under his covers. Grandpop Barley,
seated a safe distance away, raised his eyes to the ceiling.

I'll take that as a yes. The spine of the book opened with a crack, ·

and some dust spurted up into the air. I coughed and waved it away. *If this is Mrs. Greene's favorite, then why does it look as if it hasn't been opened in fifty years?*

I cleared my throat and scooted closer to the bed. "Peter and Wendy. By J. M. Barrie. Chapter One." The print was small and faded. I held the book up to the lamplight. "'All children, except one, grow up …'"

Cliff listened with alert eyes, considering every word. Whenever we read, he always lay back on the pillows with his hands clutching the sheets until his knuckles grew white. Clutching the sheets must have worn him out, because by the end of a half-hour of reading, he was usually sound asleep.

This time, his eyelids were still fluttering when I closed the book. I sat on the floor in silence for several minutes, thinking over what I had read. The thought had never occurred to me. *To never grow up …*

"Scarlett?" Cliff murmured.

I jolted to attention. "Yes?"

Cliff blinked and yawned. "It did have stars in it. I thought it might."

"Second star to the right and straight on til morning."

"What do you think it would be like …" A smile glowed on Cliff's half-awake face. "To fly? If I could fly, I'd fly to Jupiter. And then I'd fly all the way through all the stars and the Milky Way and see all the planets. And then you know what I'd do?"

"No, I don't. What would you do?"

Cliff closed his eyes and rolled over so that he faced the wall. "I'd fly back home," he murmured. "And take you with me."

I stared at him until I saw his sheets begin to rise and fall heavily. My eyes were stinging with tears. "I'd like to go with you," I whispered.

Grandpop Barley gave a loud snort. I whipped around to see him doubled over in the armchair, sound asleep.

I rolled my eyes. *Oh, great.* Rubbing his shoulders, I tried to wake him as quietly as possible. "Come on, Grandpop Barley. We've got to get you upstairs."

He blinked at me. "Oh, good, Scarlett. You're awake. I wanted to ask you …"

I helped him out of the chair and led him down the hall. "This way," I whispered.

Grandpop Barley's voice was heavy with sleep. "What you read about maps in the mind. Is that true?"

I grunted under his heavy weight. *I've just got to make it up the stairs.* "No, Grandpop. It's just a book."

"Oh." He sighed. "I would like to see my mind map. I would like to know where it leads."

I paused in the doorway of his bedroom. "Okay, now you've already got your pajamas on, so do you think you can go to bed by yourself?"

Grandpop Barley nodded and disappeared.

A door opened downstairs, and I could hear Mama and Dad's voices in the hallway. Dad's was loud—angry. Things sounded stressful. *As usual.*

I leaned against the railing at the top of the steps, trying to make out their conversation. Dad was complaining about something to do with the new governor. I leaned forward a little bit more. The wood groaned beneath me, and the railing wobbled. *Whoa.* I took a step back, away from the unsteady rail. *Well, it's obviously not safe enough to eavesdrop from here.* The thought crossed my mind again that I needed to tell Dad to fix that the banister, but I tromped down the steps instead and into the kitchen. I was going to face them head on.

They looked up when I entered the kitchen, and I froze. I cleared my throat. "How was the meeting?"

Dad looked up with tired eyes. He shook his head. "Not good."

Mama was pulling off her sweater. She opened the refrigerator and grabbed a carton. "Milk?"

"Sure." I sat at the table across from Dad and watched as Mama poured a glass for me. Then she kissed my cheek. "You need to go to bed, Scarlett. Good night."

I drank the milk in one gulp and gave her a quick squeeze back. "Night." Then I pushed away from the table and left the kitchen. Dad began arguing again as soon as I started climbing the stairs.

"But, Vida, we've got to give this man money. I just know that, with him as our governor, things will get better."

"Things will not get better, Bill! Things are going to get worse. I keep telling you …"

I blotted them out of my mind. My hand draped across the stair rail, running the length of the smooth wood. All the thoughts in my head felt jumbled up and confusing. I thought back to what Mrs. Greene had said about God taking away hopelessness and giving peace. Every time I tried to pray, I just felt more confused. Like I was talking to thin air. Nothing ever changed.

Juli was knocked out on her bed, her face buried in the pillows. I switched on the lamp and looked her over as I undressed. She was still wearing the same brightly colored dress and her hair was a rat's nest. Her hands clutched the pillow like she was caught in some bad dream.

I felt sorry for my sister. She looked scared and alone and sad. *Just like Mama and Dad, I guess.*

I pulled off my shoes and climbed into bed, turning off the lamp. *Maybe getting sad is part of growing up. I guess that's why Peter Pan was so scared. Because things change, and you can't stop them from changing.*

I swallowed. *Maybe that's why Cliff is the only happy one in the house. Maybe one day I'll grow up and become unhappy just like everyone else, and he'll be the only lucky one left.*

The room suddenly felt cold and empty. I tucked the blankets under my chin. My thoughts ran back to Cliff and the look on his face when I was reading the story. He laughed and frowned at all the right parts like he understood Peter completely. Somewhere in his strange childlike mind, Cliff understood Neverland. And it made me want to understand it too.

My eyelids fluttered closed, and the bedroom became a wonderland in my mind. I was soaring through the stars with Cliff, and I was so close to reaching the moon. I wasn't caught between childhood and adulthood or money and poverty or any of that other complicated stuff. I was just *flying*. And it felt so good.

Chapter 10

The skirt's netting scratched at my bare legs. I pulled at the green cotton, making a face. "Mama!" I shouted. "This dress is really itchy!"

"I don't care! You're wearing it to the party, and that's that!"

Ugh. I glanced back in the mirror, turning to see if my outfit looked better from the back. *Not really.*

The dress was a green with a small sunflower print. The skirt was wide and full and stuffed with netted crinoline. A wide yellow sash hugged my waist and tied into a large bow in the back. It had been Juli's dress four years ago, and unfortunately I was still skinny enough to fit into it.

Why don't I ever get any new party dresses? An irritated feeling settled in my stomach, making my cheeks hot.

I stepped closer to the mirror to examine my face. My hair was down, but at least it was decent-looking for once. The auburn waves stayed closer to my head instead of poufing out into a frizzy mess. Actually, it looked kind of pretty if I turned just the right way.

My cheekbones were high and covered in a light dusting of freckles. The small indent was still there, the one that Frank said was an angel's kiss. *I guess it always will be there.* I brushed a finger across it before lowering my hand.

I wasn't very beautiful, especially compared to Juli, but I wasn't really ugly either, or even plain. I was just pretty enough not to be pitied and just ordinary enough not to be noticed. Mama always said I had beautiful eyes, though. They were that same sea-green color of my dress and framed by thick lashes. When Cliff was a toddler, he would ask why I had "ocean eyes," while everyone else's were just plain brown.

"Scarlett!" Mama shouted, jolting me from my thoughts.

"Coming!" I pulled on a pair of dressy sandals and straightened my sash. Then I bolted down the stairs to join my family waiting by the door.

Cliff held the picnic basket containing three peach pies. He was beaming, his hair brushed back. Juli was also waiting, with a smirk on her face. Almost all of the blue had faded from her hair, leaving it a streaky gray-brown color.

"Are we ready?" Dad held open the door and shooed us out. "Come on, it's only Independence Day once a year."

The party had already started by the time we got there. Clad in breezy pink chiffon, Mrs. Greene greeted us at the door of her house. "Oh, are these the pies? I've been looking forward to them all day." She took the basket and set it on a picnic table then waved her arm to the scenery. "Enjoy!"

It hit me that I hadn't been in the Greenes' backyard since the chicken incident. The wire fence and coop were gone, and the grass was green and lush. A small creek I hadn't noticed as much before ran through the back, surrounded by large leafy trees and a few scattered picnic tables. Most of the guests had already arrived and were chatting in the warm sunlight.

Frank saw us from across the yard and waved us over. "Pretty dress," he said, looking me over with a smile. My face flushed with pleasure. He rubbed Cliff's head, messing up his perfect hair. "Hey, there."

Cliff glared at him and tried in vain to smooth his hair back into place. "Hey, watch it." He scowled, his brow puckering. Sticking his hands into his pockets, he began to rock back and forth. "What does the voice inside your head sound like? Mine is deep and smooth with a slight Spanish accent."

Frank ignored him; his eyes darted over to where the rest of my family stood. "So Juli's here."

It was more of a statement than a question. I followed his eyes to where Juli stood frowning over a grill with her arms crossed. She was arguing with the man barbecuing, probably over the skewered animal's life or something. Even though her hair was streaky, she still looked pretty fine in her golden sundress and wooden sandals. Unique—different from any of the other girls in sleepy old Georgia.

My skin felt prickly as I watched Frank watch Juli. I grabbed his arm and led him away, chatting all the while. "Doesn't the sun feel glorious? Sometimes I wish I could just float on the surface of the water like a blade of grass and feel the heat of the sun on my face and the coolness of the water on my back."

Frank glanced at me and raised an eyebrow. "You know, you say the strangest things sometimes."

I couldn't tell if that was supposed to be a compliment or an insult. My face heated. I lowered my eyes and dropped his arm. We were at the edge of the little creek watching the water break and ripple over the smooth rocks. Behind us, laughter and voices filled the yard.

A small pink flower floated on the surface of the water. It twirled slowly, drifting down the creek. So lovely and so innocent. *I wonder what Frank's thinking about.* I glanced up at him. He was staring back at the party, a smile hidden in the corner of his mouth.

I followed his gaze. Juli. She was laughing. Laughing at something the barbecuing, animal-skewering man was saying. Her face came alive when she laughed; her eyes crinkled and dimples appeared in the middle of her cheeks.

Frank turned to me. "I, uh, think I'm going to get something to drink. Or eat. You know." He flashed me one of his hundred-watt smiles and rejoined the party.

I was left standing by myself at the water's edge. My cheeks felt cold all of a sudden, all the blood drained from them. I wrapped my arms around my chest, covering the cheerful sunflowers on my dress. *I'm so childish. So scrawny and babyish.*

"Knock, knock."

Cliff's voice broke through my thoughts. I looked down to see him standing by my side, hands in his pockets. I groaned. "Not now, Cliff."

"Knock, knock," he said again, more persistent this time.

He obviously wasn't going to leave until he got his joke out. "Who's there?"

"Tank."

"Tank who?"

"You're welcome!" He burst into giggles like this was the funniest thing ever.

"Nice." I faked a smile and looked away.

Cliff's mood suddenly turned serious and he sighed as if something heavy had been weighing on his mind. "You know, I've been thinking. Peter Pan would be able to get to Neverland much faster if he used rocket power. Now, I haven't got the whole thing figured out yet, but they could build a rocket big enough for all of the Lost Boys and Wendy, John, and Michael—and Peter could be the captain! It would get there in no time and there would be less danger of pirates shooting them down." He grinned until his cheeks looked ready to burst. "Pirates can't hit something flying at rocket speed."

I sighed. "Cliff, what happened to Grandpop Barley? Is he with Mama and Dad?"

An injured look washed over Cliff's face. He crossed his arms. "Hey, haven't you been listening to me?"

My head began to hurt. I rubbed it and forced a smile. "Yeah, I'm sorry. Sounds great." I began walking back toward the party. Cliff fell into step beside me, and I turned his way. "So are you going to pilot your rocket to Neverland now?"

He shook his head. "It's not real."

I blinked. "Oh, and so you're really going to Jupiter?"

"Of course!"

I swallowed a laugh. "Oh. Okay."

When we got closer to the rest of the group, I noticed Grandpop Barley was standing by one of the many picnic tables and talking with Pastor Greene. One hand firmly clutched the end of his red tie, while the other was casually stuffed in his pocket. "Yes, siree, Reverend. Things are a-changing, I hope. Someday it'll be different." His face cracked into a smile. "Just you wait and see."

Pastor Greene looked up as we approached. "Oh, hello, Scarlett and Cliff. I'm so glad your family could join us. Beautiful weather, isn't it?" He glanced up at the sky. "I was just talking to your grandfather here about when he was a boy. In fact …" Looking around to see if anyone could hear, he leaned in and whispered something in Grandpop's ear.

Grandpop Barley's eyebrows shot up. "Where?"

Pastor Greene pointed in reply, motioning toward the edge of the house. Grandpop Barley smiled again and made a beeline in that direction.

Cliff frowned and turned toward Pastor Greene. "What did you tell him?"

"I told him that Mrs. Ima Nice had just arrived." He lifted a pitcher. "Lemonade?"

I let him pour a glass for me and took a big sip, enjoying the sugary relief. I licked my lips. "Why is he so interested in her?" I still couldn't figure out his sudden attraction to Mrs. Nice.

Pastor Greene cleared his throat. His brown eyes squinted from the sun. "Because Ima Nice, or Ima Kilpatrick as she was known then, used to be his sweetheart. Apparently, everyone thought they would marry back in the spring of 1917, but I guess one of them called it off." He cleared his throat. "I think it may have had to do with the difference in backgrounds. Anyway, Mrs. Nice married a stock broker from New York, and your grandfather worked on a peach farm for the next five years until he met your grandmother."

I frowned. "How do you know that?" *Has he been investigating our family history or something?*

Pastor Greene wiggled his eyebrows. "Mrs. Nice tells me a lot on my pastoral visits. She's really a sweet lady deep down inside. And she loved your grandfather very, very much."

"Oh." So he used to have it bad for Mrs. Nice. That would explain his infatuation with her the other afternoon. *Grandpop Barley in love.*

"Hey, I didn't know Frank was friends with Juli."

Cliff's words jolted me to attention. I blinked, following his pointed finger. Frank and Juli were standing by the water's edge, talking. They bent their heads toward each other as if sharing some secret. Smiles glowed on both their faces.

Everything inside me stung. That's where he and I were just standing. *How can he stand there with her and feel everything, but when it's me beside him he feels nothing at all?*

"I'm going to try and find some Doritos," Cliff said, wiggling his eyebrows. "Maybe they'll have some!" He darted off, scurrying past people and leaving a wake of whispers behind him.

I carried my glass of lemonade and stood by the fence where I wouldn't be noticed. Then I leaned against the weathered wood and watched the party. I observed old people bickering, young people laughing, and children running around. But mostly, I watched Frank and Juli.

He loves her. He doesn't even know her, and he loves her. The thought bothered me beyond rationality. *Why should I care? Why should it bother me that though they know absolutely nothing about each other, they're standing there and ...* Oh! The thought made me want to kick something.

"Penny for your thoughts."

I looked up to see Mrs. Greene with a giant slice of peach pie. She lifted her fork and pointed it at me. "I just thought I'd come over and tell you how delicious this is."

"Thanks," I muttered, lowering my gaze.

Mrs. Greene leaned against the fence beside me and let out a long, leisurely sigh. Then she turned to me. "What's bothering you, Scarlett? Something's wrong."

I shrugged. "It's nothing."

"Uh-huh." She nodded toward Frank and Juli. "They seem happy together, don't they?"

A rush of pressure built up in my chest. "Well, they shouldn't be! Juli already has a boyfriend. And they know nothing about each other."

Mrs. Green raised an eyebrow. She slowly lifted another forkful of pie to her lips and chewed while I stood in shameful silence. *Nice outburst, Scarlett. Real nice.*

"Does it bother you? Them being together, I mean."

I shrugged and turned, folding my arms on the fencepost. "I don't see why it should."

"But it does."

Something snapped inside of me. "Yes." I whipped around, my hair stinging my face. "It does. Because Frank loves Juli, and I don't think she'll ever love him back. Because she doesn't even know him. She doesn't know about the sparkle in his eyes when he talks about his animals or the way he chews on his lip when he can't get something straight or the way he laughs and shakes his head at the same time." I refolded my arms. "The only thing she probably notices is how nice his shiny hair looks in the sun."

Mrs. Greene pursed her lips like she was trying to disguise a smile. She placed the plate of pie on the fence. "So I was right. You like him. Even more than that, you love him. Right?"

It felt as if a thunderbolt cracked through me and got trapped in my body. *What? That's.... That's crazy. Totally and utterly crazy. Complete nonsense. Completely ...*

"Yes," I moaned, burying my face in my hands. "He's crazy and insane sometimes, and he's head over heels in love with my sister, but I'm the stupid girl who wants to be with him."

"I see."

A painful silence followed. My chest felt like it was caving in from shame and anger and something close to wonder. Wonder at how completely foolish and stubborn my love for him was. Wonder at how that love was still there despite what was in front of me.

"Well, he's going to college in the fall, correct?"

My head snapped back up. *Going to college.* He was leaving, probably for good, at the end of the summer. A wild feeling clawed at me. "What do I do?"

Mrs. Greene licked some peach juice from her finger and looked at me squarely. "You tell him how you feel. Tell him that you love him and want to be with him when he returns. Provided he feels the same way you do, and you both still feel the same way after you're both done with school, you can think about marrying and settling down." She raised an eyebrow. "Just don't get too carried away. You're still years and years away from being old enough for even thinking about all that matrimony stuff, right?"

I glanced back at Frank. Would he want to marry me? Could a perfectly impetuous boy like Frank Leggett want to marry the sister of the girl he's pined over for years? I turned back, my chest deflated. "Frank loves Juli."

"Phoo. He only *thinks* he loves Juli. They're not meant for each other. Juli is headstrong and brash. She won't be tamed for many more years, and most likely it will be by a strong and rugged stranger." Mrs. Greene's hand reached out and touched my own ever so gently. "You don't have to tell him how you feel. You can stay perched in your birdcage forever." Her voice softened. "Or you can *fly*."

Chapter 11

It was just after twelve o'clock, and the sun was already making my skin melt and my dress stick to my back. I fanned myself with a napkin I'd found lying around and squinted down the road. No sign of Frank.

Cliff was sitting on the ground with a pad of paper and a pen. From time to time, he'd hold it up and show me what he was working on. It was usually an elaborate spaceship of some kind.

"Peter Pan is going to be my copilot," he said out loud, furiously coloring in the sparks beneath the rocket. He glanced up and frowned. "Or would it be co-astronaut? Are astronauts called pilots sometimes?"

"I don't know." I pressed my lips together and looked again toward the direction of Frank's house. Nothing.

We could technically head back into the house anytime we wanted. We'd been selling pies since nine, and we only had one left. Plus, we had agreed in the beginning that we wouldn't stay out too long in the heat. Georgia afternoon heat waves can be killers.

But Frank hadn't showed up yet. It didn't make any sense. He was always there by nine. Ten, at the latest. Here it was quarter past twelve and no sign of him.

I squirmed in my seat and stared at the pie sitting in front of me. Flaky bits of crust clung to the red gingham tablecloth covering the stand. I scraped a bit of peach goop off the side of the pie and stuck my finger into my mouth. A weird mixture of salty sweat and sticky sugar.

Maybe he found out about my conversation with Mrs. Greene last Friday. I racked my brain to think if I'd seen him since then. I hadn't. He'd left the party saying something about a boating trip his family was taking this week, but he'd assured me that he'd be back in time to sell pies today. That was eight days ago. What if someone told him since then about what I said?

Who else would know? That was a comforting thought. No one else was nearby, right? There was no way he would know. It was between me and Mrs. Greene.

There was a loud ripping sound as Cliff tore his picture off of the pad of paper and handed it to me. "Here you go! We can put this by the sale sign. Then, if anyone comes, I can explain to them about how this is Peter Pan and this is Captain Cliff and we're going to Jupiter together."

But if he didn't know, why else would he not come? I scratched at a bug bite on my leg.

Maybe Frank was getting tired of us.

It made sense, in a way. It's not like we were the most stimulating people to be around. Cliff was in some kind of delusional world ninety percent of the time, referring to himself in third person and chastising me in a weird mixture of English and Spanish. And I certainly wasn't as pretty or interesting as Juli.

My stomach sank. He was sick of being around us. Now that Juli had noticed him, Frank probably realized he could attract the attention of much more fascinating people. After all, part of our deal had been I would introduce him to my sister.

I looked back down the road one more time. No more cars or people, which made sense. We'd always told customers that we were closing at twelve, before the day got too hot. Usually we took a break between twelve and three and then reopened at four when the air was a bit cooler.

"Come on, Cliff." I stood and stretched trying to seem as nonchalant as possible. "Let's go in the house. We'll bring this pie out this evening and see if we can sell it."

He scampered to his feet and pulled together all of his drawing supplies. Then he proceeded to talk my ear off about Jupiter and Peter Pan all the way back up the driveway.

Not that I was really listening. I was walking, one foot in front of the other, toward the house with only one thing on my mind: Frank.

I wasn't even that upset that he didn't care for me or didn't want to be with me. It was more than that. Frank was the only person who had ever seemed to look past our eccentricities and labels to see the *real* Cliff and Scarlett. I'd never known him to think that we were weirdos or oddballs like everyone else seemed to. He saw our flaws and quirks and still liked us in spite of them.

Well, at least, I *thought* he liked us. I thought he was our friend. Friends are supposed to be steady, dependable but I hadn't heard from Frank in over a week. I knew he and his family were home—I'd seen their car when I biked past there yesterday. But something was keeping him away. And I was determined to find out what that was.

"You go on into the house," I told Cliff. "I'm going to ride over to the orchard and pick up some more peaches."

Cliff's face lit up. "Oh! I want to come! I can't wait to tell Frank how—"

"No!"

My word cut through the air like a knife, stopping Cliff midsentence. He frowned, his brows drawing together. He opened his mouth then slowly shut it. "Okay," he mumbled, trudging up the steps.

Standing alone on the front porch, I wrapped my arms around my chest. Suddenly, the ninety-five-degree heat didn't seem so warm anymore.

The wind kissed my cheeks as I pedaled toward Frank's house, making my hair fly behind me. The air slid down the back of my dress, cooling my skin. *At least I won't show up in his orchard with a sticky back.*

For a glorious four and a half minutes, it felt like I was flying. Georgia sped past me, the neighborhood houses as well as nearby orchards and farm houses blurring in my side vision. It was close to mid-July, and many crops were reaching full ripeness, leaving a mingling of sweet Southern laziness and overflowing fruitfulness in the air.

I closed my eyes for a second and imagined that wings pulled me through the air. I felt weightless, happy, free.

Mrs. Greene's words rang in my ears. *"You can stay perched in your birdcage forever. Or you can fly."*

Fly. The word was so appealing. Sometimes, I knew exactly how Cliff felt when he dreamed about flying to Jupiter. Out of this world, away from this mundane life. For me that meant being free from the responsibilities and pressures of growing up. Able to smooth out the tangle of thoughts and fears that always seemed to jumble up whenever I talked to Juli or Frank or Mrs. Greene.

My thoughts came tumbling down as I pulled into the Leggetts' driveway and skidded to a stop. Our family seemed so cracked lately. And I was the only glue keeping us together. Juli was defiant; Grandpop Barely was erratic; Cliff was ... well, *Cliff*; and Mama and Dad seemed dangerously close to breaking.

I was nowhere near being ready to fly.

Dropping my bike by the fence, I brushed off my knees and looked up. The Leggetts' pickup truck was sitting in the driveway. *I guess that means they're home.* That didn't really give me any indication of where Frank might be, though.

Why did I care about him anyway? I didn't, that's what.

I untied my basket from the front of my bike and headed toward the peach orchard. Frank had said that we could pick peaches any-time we needed to. We just had to let him know later.

Well, I'll let him know the next time he actually shows up to some-thing. I'm not going to go out of my way to find him just to let him know I picked a few more peaches. Besides, I have to get home and get a few more pies made before this evening anyway.

I turned just in time to see Frank climbing over the fence and into the orchard with a fluffy white cat in his hands. He shook his head, confused. "What are you doing here?"

"Peaches." I held my basket up dumbly, wanting to snatch the word up and shove it back into my mouth. Obviously, I was getting peaches. This wasn't a baked-potato orchard, for heaven's sake.

"I saw you from the house." He nodded toward where his home sat on top of the little hill, flanked by peach trees in every direction.

"Oh." I kept my gaze low. It felt awkward to look at him and talk to him in light of last week's sudden realization.

But Frank didn't seem bothered. He sat down at the base of one of the peach trees and stroked the white cat. "This is Monica," he said, rubbing her head. She ducked and rubbed her nose against his neck, clearly infatuated. "A family who lived about five minutes down the road recently moved away. They asked me if I'd take care of her, so I said yes. She's only been here about a week, but she seems pretty happy." He chuckled, tickling the cat under the chin. His golden eyelashes brushed his cheeks before glancing up at me.

I pressed my lips together and tucked a piece of hair behind my ear. "Why 'Monica'?"

"Why not?"

He had me smiling then, so I sat next to him and rested the bas-ket of peaches on my lap. It was cooler in the shade, and the flies were more preoccupied with the fallen fruit than our skin. So it was nice.

"Besides," Frank said, "Cliff wasn't around to throw out any Spanish names."

"I bet he could have come up with some good ones."

"Yeah. No doubt about it."

I rested my head against the bark of the tree and picked up a peach. Turning it over in my hands, the pink fuzz tickled my skin. I gave it a little squeeze. *Just ripe enough.*

"Oh, darn!" Frank sat up straight, startling Monica. She jumped out of his lap and flicked her tail, trotting away.

Frank glanced at me nervously and ran a hand through his hair. "I completely forgot about the stand today, Scarlett."

I shrugged. *Hopefully, this comes across as nonchalant, rather than stinging of injured pride.* "It's fine. We were fine."

"No, it's not. I promised you I'd be there." He picked a twig off the ground and poked at his arm. His skin was so tan from the summer sun that it nearly matched the brown of the wood. "I was filling out college applications, and I just lost track of the day and time."

"College?" My voice came out squeaky, but he didn't seem to notice.

"Yeah. I'm applying at Georgia Tech and Boston University."

"Boston?" *Boston?* As in the Massachusetts kind of Boston? All the US geography maps I'd memorized in grade school came rushing back to me. That was a completely different part of the country.

Frank's smile had faded. He was poking at his arm more energetically now, hardly grimacing at the tiny marks the twig left in his skin. "They have an incredible track for aspiring veterinarians. It would be amazing." He sighed. "But I doubt I'll even get accepted. And I know that my parents want me to go to Georgia Tech, and that's where I'll probably end up going, but still."

I wasn't sure if I wanted to say this, because I wanted him to stay in Georgia forever, but I swallowed and pressed forward. "Frank, what do *you* want to do?"

He tilted his head down. "I don't know if that matters all that much. Dad wants me to be a businessman. To own peach farms and real estate like he does. Or go to law school and be a lawyer or doctor or something." He shrugged. "Anything that will make me rich and bitter in the end, I suppose."

The way his brow furrowed and his shoulders slumped made my heart break. My chest ached to find the right words to say to make him smile and laugh. Instead I sat beside him silent, like a tongue-tied fool. I didn't know much about law school or owning peach farms, but I did wonder how Frank could become a doctor with his grades. I guess he was smart enough to do whatever he wanted, no matter what scores were on his tests. He looked me in the face. "Sometimes I just feel so trapped here. I don't want to grow up and live my whole life in this one little town. And everyone—my mom, my dad, my teachers—everyone seems to want to stick me in some kind of … I don't know …"

"Cage."

"What?"

"They want to put you in a cage," I said, my voice soft. "They're afraid to let you fly."

"Yes! That's exactly how I feel!" Frank shook his head, as if I'd just said the most incredulous thing. He bit his lip and nodded. "I don't want to have to stay in this cage forever. I don't have anything holding me back. Why can't they just let me fly?"

I certainly had things holding me back. Cliff, Grandpop Barley, Juli, Mama, and Dad. My whole family.

For a split second, I felt green with envy. If Frank was in a cage, it certainly wasn't one that would hold him for very long. He could easily pack up and move to Boston if he wanted to. No one would be able to keep him grounded.

But that wasn't the case for me. I could leave Georgia tomorrow, put all my belongings in a suitcase, and hop on a train headed north. But I'd never be able to live with myself. I'd never put to rest the fact that I was abandoning my family. They needed me.

"You know, that's what I love about Juli," Frank was saying, a pleasant look finally spreading across his face. "She's just so carefree and independent. She wouldn't care about what college her parents wanted her to go to. She'd just go wherever she pleased and be happy about it."

Again with Juli. My chest panged.

"I'd care." I placed the peach basket on the ground next to me and pulled my knees up to my chest, wrapping my arms around them. "I'd care what my parents thought."

"What do you mean?" Frank's voice was soft.

"It would break my heart if I did something that hurt my mother. If I left her." I bit the inside of my cheek. The sun was blazing through the leaves of the peach trees and shining in my eyes. "At the end of my life, it doesn't matter what college is on my diploma. Or what state I'm living in or what job I've retired from."

I took a deep breath. "If my family falls apart, everything else does too. And I'd never be able to fall asleep at night with the memory of walking away and leaving them behind." My voice grew small. "I need them just as much as they need me."

Frank blinked at me. Silence spread between us in the muggy air. He leaned forward until his face was less than a foot away. Then he licked his lips and whispered, "You're nothing like Juli, are you?"

"No."

Frank let out a breath and straightened. "I guess you're right. Come on." He climbed to his feet and brushed off his jeans before helping me up. "Well, I think it's getting too late to make those extra pies. Why don't you stay for supper instead? I'll ask my mom, but I'm sure it will be okay."

"No." I wrapped a thick strand of hair around my finger and made a face. "I really do have to get home. Mama got called into the plantation this afternoon, and there's no one else to make supper."

Frank's eyebrows rose. "You really do it all, don't you?"

I shrugged and picked up the peach basket. "Someone has to." Tucking it under my arm, I waved lamely and started walking toward my bike. Back to my world of weird, eccentric, crazy normality, the one I both loved and loathed in turns.

● ● ●

"Shhh! It's coming on!" Cliff kicked at my legs under the blanket.

I giggled and kicked back. "You're so excited."

"Hush, you two!" Grandpop Barley's voice cut short our laughter. We glanced at each other and blinked, before bursting back into giggles.

Our eyes were glued to the small television screen. Because, once again, we were viewing the moon from our attic. Only this time, men had landed on it.

Cliff's body felt tense beside me. Every muscle in him seemed clenched, waiting in anticipation for that moment when a man would step onto the moon.

My fingers clutched at the blanket. The door of the hatch was opening. "Do you think that's really happening?" I whispered. "That right now men are climbing out into space?"

"Shh," he hissed.

The door opened completely and a large marshmallow-like figure stepped out.

"That's astronaut Neil Armstrong," Cliff whispered.

"I know." I tossed a pillow at him, causing him to duck. "The man from NASA just said that."

"Hey, don't throw things at me!"

"Just watch!"

Neil Armstrong was speaking. As he climbed down the ladder, he described the surface of the moon below, and then, finally, he stepped all the way down. I gasped softly as Walter Cronkite confirmed someone was actually *walking* on the moon. "That's one small step for man, one giant leap for mankind." Armstrong's voice sounded crackly and far away.

Cliff squealed and looked at me. "He's walking. On the moon!"

"I know!"

Cliff's face was practically luminescent. He turned back to the television fixated on what was unfolding on the screen.

The footage was fuzzy and blurred, and I couldn't help think the astronauts looked a lot like wavering moonbeams, iridescent and shiny. They bopped around on the moon as if their bodies were full of air.

"I was really hoping they'd be able to fly out there." Cliff looked a little disappointed. "I thought that once you were in outer space, you could fly."

I bit my lip. "Well, it looks like they're tied down. Maybe they'd float away if they were loose. That's kind of like flying, right?"

Cliff's eyebrows rose. "Yeah."

"A hoax!" Grandpop Barley *harrumphed* from his seat in the armchair. "The whole thing is a phony scheme! Man can't be on the moon. He couldn't survive! He couldn't breathe!"

A vein rose on Cliff's forehead. "That's not true!" He stood, clutching one of Grandpop Barley's pillows to his chest. "You're lying! They really are on the moon!"

"Cliff!" I jumped up and wrestled the pillow out of his hand. "Sit down!"

Reluctantly, Cliff sat, a scowl wiped across his once-happy face. Exasperated, I rubbed my forehead and shot Grandpop Barley a glare. "If the US government says that they're on the moon, don't you think they're on the moon?"

He grunted and shook his head, leaning back to close his eyes.

I sighed and settled back into my place on the floor. *Only Grandpop Barley could make the moon landing into a family squabble.*

Chapter 12

It was a hot day, the kind that sweltered and boiled near the end of summer. My hair fluttered in the wind, whipping all around me like a living thing. Georgia whizzed by, until I swerved my bike to avoid hitting a turtle that was stranded in the middle of the road. *Poor little thing. The pond's a whole twenty feet away.*

My mouth twitched. *I should help it.* I skidded on the brakes.

"Scarlett!"

I jolted. The edge of my front tire caught on a rock, sending me and my bike tumbling over into the dirt. I landed in a heap of tangled curls and jumbled limbs. *Oh no.* I buried my face in the grass. *Please don't tell me that was …*

"Are you okay?"

My eyes slid shut. *Of course, Frank saw me flip over a rock and land with my face in the mud.*

He was by my side in an instant, gently cupping my elbows. "Wow, that looked really painful. Are you … Is anything broken?"

I pushed myself to my knees and rubbed my arms. "Would it be cliché to say, 'Only my pride'?"

Frank laughed, shaking his head. "Yeah."

I looked up with a smile and realized with a startling jolt that he was sitting inches away from me and looked concerned about my scrapes but happy about my intact sense of humor. *Shouldn't it make me all fluttery inside to think that I love him and he's sitting next to me, smiling at me like that?* But I didn't feel fluttery at all, just warm and easy. Like this was the way it was supposed to be. To love someone and feel completely happy and relaxed. It was just that simple.

Frank lifted a hand and brushed the veil of hair away from my face, tucking it behind my ear. I was close enough to smell the soap on his skin and to see the golden specks in his eyes. In his eyes that were looking right at me and smiling like he knew being together like this was easy too.

The corner of Frank's mouth twitched upward. He reached out and helped pull me up. "I'm surprised Cliff's not around to be the cause of this mishap."

"Oh, no. He's home right now. I was just biking around and enjoying the sunshine when …" *The turtle!* I jumped up, grabbing Frank's sleeve. "I hope he's still alive! I don't think I hit him."

"What? Hit who?"

I pulled Frank back over to the road, where the turtle had balled up into his shell again. I knelt on the ground and stroked the warm, sunbathed surface. I squinted up at Frank. "We should probably get it back to the pond where it can cool off."

He nodded. "I'll grab it," he said, scooping up the turtle.

My eyes widened, and I took a step forward. I didn't think you were supposed to just pick up turtles. "What if it's a snapping …"

Frank suddenly threw his hand back. I screamed, trembling mid-sentence. Frank held up the hand, an impish smile on his face. No bite marks. No blood.

"Just kidding."

"That wasn't funny." I broke into laughter all the same. Because it was kind of funny.

"Sure it was." Frank knelt by the edge of the pond and placed the turtle in the water. He stood and wiped his hands off on his jeans. "I don't think I've ever heard you scream before. But, seriously, you're really good at it. You should audition for one of those bad horror movies. You know, the ones where the beautiful girls scream their heads off because some mutant beaver maimed a guy's hand?"

I shook my head. "You're so weird."

"No, you'd be great!" Frank crossed his heart. "Upon my honor."

My bike was still lying in the middle of the road. I lifted it and inspected the front. No dents. I touched the spot where my ribs smashed into the handlebars and winced. *That'll hurt tomorrow.*

"I never figured I'd be an actress," I said as I pushed the battered bike back toward home. Frank fell into step beside me and shoved his hands into his pockets. "I don't have a face for the big screen. Juli maybe, but never me."

"What?" Frank snorted. "That's the stupidest thing I've ever heard. Your face could hold its own alongside John Wayne or Paul Newman. You're one of the prettiest girls in Georgia, I think."

My face heated. I glanced at him sideways, to see if he was joking. He looked away quickly and stared at the road ahead of us. *Oh.* A smile spread across my face.

● ● ●

Before I realized it, we were standing by my mailbox. I propped my bike up against the gate and sighed. "You know, I wasn't planning on coming home for a while."

"Really?" Frank smiled. He shrugged and stuck his hands in his pockets. "We can go to the peach orchard, if you want." He cleared his throat. "Only if, you know, you don't have any other plans."

I grinned. "Sure. Race you there?"

He nodded and took off, leaving me to chase after him. We both reached the orchard at the same time. With my heart slamming against my chest, I leaned on the fence and tried to catch my breath. Frank settled himself on the ground and laid out on his back. I sat beside him and watched the clouds sail across the ocean-blue sky.

"Would you rather ride a cloud or a raindrop?" Frank asked, glancing at me.

"A cloud. I hate being wet."

"Huh." He looked back up at the sky. "Yeah, me too, I think."

I pressed my lips together. "Would you rather fall out of an airplane and discover you can fly, or sink in a boat and discover you can breathe underwater?"

"Fly."

"Definitely."

"Right." Frank's mouth twitched. "Would you rather eat cake every morning for breakfast, or pie every day for lunch?"

I laughed. "Why is it boys always think about food?"

"Just answer."

"Okay, fine. Pie. I really like pie."

"Me too."

Frank turned and looked at me again, the gold in his eyes matching the hair that fell on his forehead. And once again it felt so simple to be sitting beside him and talking. It felt *right*.

"You know," Frank said softly, "I think you're the closest to a best friend I've ever had."

"Me too," I said. But what I was really thinking was that I didn't want to just be Frank's best friend. I wanted to marry him and grow old with him and sit and talk with him forever. But every time I opened my mouth to say so, I found it was frozen shut.

Besides, Frank loves Juli. Juli, with the perfect smile and wild streak and dangerous balance of sane and insane. Juli, who was more desirable than me in so many ways.

I pushed myself up. Suddenly, the sun felt too hot and the air too humid and all the things that were left unsaid between us were just too much to handle. "I should really go. I remembered I promised Cliff I'd play Spanish Civil War with him this afternoon. This time he gets to be the guerrillas."

"Fun." Frank stood and stuck his hands back into his pockets. His forehead was pinched in confusion, but he nodded. "Well, I guess I'll see you on Saturday, then. At the pie stand."

"Right. Okay, then. See you later." Then I turned and walked away. I wanted to be calm and cool-headed. Carefree. But my stomach was roiling. Because, as much as I wanted things to be simple and easy, I couldn't help but feel like my life was quickly becoming the most complicated one on earth.

• • •

On Friday afternoon I knocked once, but no answer. Twice, and still no footsteps coming down the hall.

That's funny. Her car is in the driveway. I stood on tiptoe and tried to peek through the frosted window by the door. A lacy curtain fell over the glass, blocking my vision.

I raised my hand to knock again when the door flew open. *What in the ...* I blinked.

Standing in front of me was Mrs. Greene. Or at least it looked like her. Sort of.

Her long blonde hair was falling down her shoulders in tangled knots. Mascara had smeared around her eyes and down her cheeks, and her pretty dress and fancy light sweater were wrinkled. She sniffed and rubbed her forehead. "Oh, I meant to tell you not to come today."

My presence on her doorstep suddenly felt very awkward. Whatever was going on, she definitely didn't need me in the middle of it. I took a step back, stumbling on the mat. "Um, okay. I'll just go."

Mrs. Greene shook her head as if trying to compose herself. "No. Come in, Scarlett."

Her voice sounded like she was stuck in a tunnel or in the early stages of a bad cold. Mrs. Greene sat and pointed to an empty barstool next to her. "We're not cooking today. I called everyone to say we wouldn't be stopping in." She sniffed again. "I thought I'd be gone."

I glanced around the kitchen. It seemed undisturbed. Everything in place, hanging neatly or stacked in the cupboards. A pair of keys lying discarded on the counter. I pressed my lips together and swung my legs under my stool, letting the silence hang in the air.

"Um, I guess you're wondering why I look like this." Her face was blotchy red under the tear streaks.

I kept my mouth shut. Obviously, I was wondering that. But it wasn't like I was going to come right out and *ask*. So I crossed my legs at the ankles and waited for her to go on.

"Today is our seven-year wedding anniversary. Tim's and mine." She let out a jagged breath and rubbed the golden band on her finger. "We've always been extravagant in our celebrating. Tim likes to give me the traditional anniversary gifts. You know, paper or wood or whatever." She pointed at the clock on the wall. "He gave me that charming cuckoo clock for our fifth anniversary."

Okay. I forced a smile. *Where's the tragedy in all this?*

Mrs. Greene sighed and pressed her hands together. "This year he was supposed to give me wool or copper, according to the chart. And so I woke up expecting to find something wrapped by the bed like usual ..." Her mouth twitched. "I got him wool slippers, although I hid them in the closet. Anyway, when there was no gift waiting for me, I thought maybe he was planning to surprise me by taking me out to lunch. So I called and canceled all the meals and got all dolled up in my best dress and piled my hair up ..."

Her voice began to deflate, and her lip quivered. Looking at me with piercingly sad eyes, she whimpered, "Scarlett, he forgot our anniversary. He didn't remember at all."

I blinked. "How could he, if you two make such a big deal out of it?"

"I don't know!" She hugged her sweater close. "It was more than just the anniversary, though. It's been like this all week. He's been so busy and always coming home late and seeming frazzled."

Should I let her talk to me like this? It wasn't like I had any advice to give her or anything. And she was the pastor's wife, for heaven's sake.

Mrs. Greene sniffled. "It got so bad that I just blew up this morning. I called his office and pouted and screamed and said the most ... horrible things." She shivered. "I told him that I didn't want to live in this house and have to sit and look at a husband who didn't care enough about his wife to make time for her, even on the most important day of the year."

My eyes widened. "You didn't."

"Yes!" Mrs. Greene moaned and buried her head on the table. "Oh, I've been a mess all afternoon. I'm so angry at him and at the same time so angry at myself."

She tried to control the tears, but her shoulders were shaking visibly. The more I watched her, the heavier my chest felt.

Why do couples have to fight all the time? And over such stupid things. A lump formed in my throat. *Why do they call it family when it isn't even strong enough to handle things like this?*

"I don't even care about copper or wool. I was just mad because he didn't remember me. I've felt so unimportant lately, Scarlett. But I was being so silly. I'm sorry you are seeing me this way. I've probably shared more than I should with you." She dropped her head and tried to compose herself.

Feeling more like an adult than a child, I reached out and began rubbing her shoulders, searching for the right thing to say to a woman who suddenly seemed so different from the one I knew.

But every time something popped into my mind, it seemed so completely wrong. So I zipped my lips and rubbed her back in silence.

The minutes dragged by slowly. My eyes wandered around the room, resting first on the cuckoo clock. It really was cute. Mrs. Greene must have been really pleased when she opened it.

I looked down at her. Her hair was silky and smooth, falling down her back in waves. *No wonder her bouffant is so high.* I thought about asking her how it fell out of its updo.

Suddenly, the door flung open. The hairs on my arm stood up. Pastor Greene stood in the doorway with a bouquet of roses in his hands. He didn't even seem to notice me as he floated through the kitchen and knelt by his wife's side.

"Dotty," he whispered, pushing back her tangled hair. He planted a kiss on her cheek and whispered something in her ear. Then he pulled out a gift from behind his back and watched her with the remorseful, anxious expression of a schoolboy. "I really didn't mean to forget. I just was so worried about other things that it slipped my mind. You know I'd never do anything to hurt you. You're the most …" He reached out and stroked her blonde hair. "You're the most beautiful, special, wonderful …"

Mrs. Greene lifted her head with gleaming eyes. She threw her arms around his neck and cut off his words with a kiss, tears still falling down her cheeks. Their kiss deepened, and they pulled each other close, completely oblivious to my presence.

I took a step back. *Just when I thought things couldn't get more awkward, I witness the pastor and his wife making out in their kitchen. Nice.* I considered announcing my departure but decided to just slip out the back door.

On the walk back home, I felt more confused than ever. Pastor and Mrs. Greene had always seemed so happy and perfect for each other, but one silly misunderstanding seemed to unravel everything. Maybe I didn't understand love at all—certainly not the love between a man and a woman. And I most certainly didn't know what to think of the idea of "divine love."

Once again, I felt caught. Caught in the middle of ignorance and knowledge, childhood and adulthood. Loneliness and happiness.

I sighed and stuck my hands in my pockets.

● ● ●

"You know what I thought of today?" Cliff tucked the covers under his chin and pulled his knees close to his chest.

"Hmm?" I flipped through the pages of *Peter and Wendy*. Where did we last stop? It had been a busy week, and I'd only had time to read to him once or twice. There didn't seem to be time for anything lately. I hadn't seen Mrs. Greene in over a week, and I'd only run into Frank once or twice in the past ten days.

"We only have one more month before school starts. Today is August eighth. Soon it'll be September."

I halted. He was right. "I guess the summer's almost over, huh?" It was a sad thought. Fall meant the end of peach stands, sweltering afternoons, and all the other things I had started to consider normal.

He nodded. "And we still haven't built our rocket."

I patted his knee. "Yeah, well, we'll do that soon. As soon as we have fifty dollars, I'll get Frank to drive us into town so we can pick out all the supplies. We'll get it done before September. Promise."

"Okay." Cliff snuggled under the blanket. "You ended with chapter eight."

"Oh, right." *How does he remember that?* I cleared my throat. "Chapter Eight. The Mermaids' Lagoon."

Cliff recited the Spanish numbers softly to himself while I read. "Uno, dos, tres …" Every now and then he'd look up and laugh at something I read.

Grandpop Barley had already fallen asleep and was snoring in the chair by the door. I tried not to think about the struggle it would take to drag him up the stairs.

When I finished the chapter, I closed the book firmly and rubbed Cliff's forehead. "Sweet dreams. Are you ready for the peach stand tomorrow?"

He nodded. "I think we'll reach fifty dollars."

"I hope so." Ruffling his hair, I turned to Grandpop Barley. "Okay. You. Up."

Chapter 13

The Saturday afternoon sun felt hot and muggy overhead, beating down on our backs. I fanned myself with a piece of paper, squinting to keep the sweat out of my eyes. Noon had already come and gone, and I was starting to think anyone who was planning on buying pies had come by already. We'd already sold five, so there was only one pie left anyway. No use in waiting around for who knows how many more hours to make a measly two dollars.

How much have we made anyway? The money jar was sitting next to me on the ground. I untwisted the cap and pulled out a bundle of cash. Flipping through it, I counted ones and fives silently. *Twenty, twenty-five, thirty ... -one ... two, three, four! Thirty-four dollars!*

I jumped out of the lawn chair and did a little happy dance. *Thirty-four dollars! Cliff is going to be over the moon!* I smirked. *Or maybe over Jupiter.*

I took the stand down in record time and sped up the driveway with the money in my pocket. A wide smile stayed plastered on my dirty, sweaty face. *We could have that rocket by this time next week!*

Cliff was sitting on the front steps with his chin resting in his hand. He looked up and frowned when he saw me. "Juli ran away."

I froze, halting midstride. "What do you mean?"

He shook his head. Lopsided curls fell across his forehead. "Juli's gone for good. She left this morning. All of her stuff is missing."

My body felt numb. *What? How could … Juli would never do this.* I raised a finger to my pulsing temple, brushing past Cliff. "I don't believe you."

I shoved open the screen door. "Mama! Dad! Cliff says …" Once again, I was stopped in my tracks. "No." My voice cracked. "It's not true."

"Scarlett." Dad sat up when he saw me come in. They were both sitting at the table holding hands. Mama's face was streaked with tears. "Did you notice what time Juli left this morning?"

My mouth felt dry. "Um, I …" I gulped. "I think she left about nine this morning. Mrs. Greene was picking up some pies, and Juli drove by in her car. I was going to wave, but she didn't look at me, and I was sure … I *am* sure that she'll be back. She'll be back, right?"

Right? The word echoed in my head, unanswered.

Dad looked up at me and said in a low, shaky voice, "Can you go upstairs and see if there's anything left on her side of the room? We need to find out where she went. Just look for … anything." He bent his head and massaged Mama's hands. "We can't bring ourselves to go up there again right now."

I backed out of the room; my head was spinning. Taking the steps two at a time, I flung open the bedroom door and stared. The room was half empty. Juli's bed lay deserted, stripped of its sheets and pillows. Her side of the closet was vacant. Her posters and pictures were missing from the wall.

A lump formed in my throat. *No. Juli would never do this. She would never just … leave. Without telling anyone. Without telling me.*

A picture flashed through my mind: Juli, looking out the front window of her car while dust swirled around me as she drove past earlier that morning. I'd glanced at her, but I hadn't really *looked*. Had she been crying? Was she mad? Was there something she was trying to tell me—to signal to me—that I'd been too blind to see?

I knelt on the floor and looked under her bed, searching for clues. Nothing. I looked in the closet, under the window, in her old chest of drawers. After ten minutes of searching, I rocked back on my heels and sighed. It was time to face the facts. Juli had left and taken everything with her.

In one last-ditch search, I found a note under my pillow that had been folded into a tiny rectangle. I opened it and smoothed out the wrinkles. There was a short sentence written in Juli's messy scrawl:

Gone with Ziggy.

—Juli

My stomach sank. Slowly trodding down the stairs, I debated what to tell Mama and Dad. If they knew she had gone with her boyfriend, they would be enraged. Sparks would fly … Voices would rise …

I shuddered. *But, on the other hand, I can't let them think she's stranded somewhere in the world with no money and no home. At least Ziggy makes a decent amount of money with his band, so we know she's not starving.*

I set my shoulders. I would show them the note. Juli would come back to Georgia soon.

With trembling hands, I passed the piece of paper to Dad. Better to let him read it first. Then he could break the news to Mama.

Dad grabbed the note so fast it almost cut my hand. His eyes squinted in concentration on the few words. He placed the paper back on the table, and a grim look settled on his face. He straightened and pushed back his chair. "She's gone with her boyfriend."

"What?" Mama's eyes bulged. She lunged for the note, as if hoping it would say something different if she read it. Her eyes skimmed the page before she collapsed in a sobbing heap on the kitchen table.

I rushed forward to rub her shoulders. "Shhh, Mama, it's okay.

I'm sure Juli's fine. She's probably feeling bad already, and she'll be back tomorrow like she always is. Just you wait and see."

Dad headed for the hall closet. That closet was never opened. Ever. All of us Blaine children were strictly forbidden to open it, and it was only to be unlatched in the case of a robbery or wild animal. Terror gripped my stomach. *That can only mean ...* I jumped up. "What are you doing?"

Without glancing at me, he opened the door and pulled out a long rifle. With a cool flick of his hand, he dusted off the barrel. "I'm going to hunt down that scoundrel. He drives a yellow Volkswagen, right? Easy. If they're driving that thing, I'm sure they haven't left the highway." He grabbed a case of bullets and made a beeline for the door.

"Bill!" Mama shrieked, lifting her head. "You're going to end up killing Juli!"

He shook his head, pulling on his boots. "I don't know who that girl thinks she is. I'll tell you what, she's going to get the punishment of her life. She is never leaving this house again!" The screen door slammed behind him.

I felt helpless, caught in the middle of a perilous spider web I didn't belong in but from which I couldn't escape. *When did things get so dramatic? What's even going on?* "Dad!" I ran out the door, racing toward the truck. *Gosh, he walks fast.* My chest felt so tight I could barely breathe. I skidded to a stop in front of him. "Don't. Just don't. Someone could get hurt," I gasped.

Dad turned, a glint of steel in his eyes. But as he looked down at me, the look softened into an expression I could only call pitiful sadness. His grip on the gun loosened until it eventually dropped in the dirt. He turned and shoved his face against the car door so I wouldn't see the tears running down his cheeks.

I picked up the gun and carried it into the house to put it back in the closet. Mama sniffled from the table. "Oh, Lord," she whispered. "It's like losing a child."

Cliff was still sitting on the front steps, watching it all. I grabbed him by the hand and pulled him up. "Come on." My voice sounded hoarse, even to my own ears. "Let's go find Grandpop Barley and go for a short walk. I think we could use it."

● ● ●

"Scarlett?" Cliff's voice sounded uneasy. He poked at my elbow, trying to get my attention. "I thought of a knock-knock joke."

I jerked my head out of my cloud of problems and tried to listen. "Yeah?"

He kicked at a rock on the side of the road. "Knock, knock."

"Who's there?" I tried to make my voice sound light. Happy.

"Wee otter."

I made a face like I was ready for a really funny one. "Wee otter who?"

"Wee otter give Mom and Dad the money."

I froze. *Where on earth did that come from?* I glanced at him to see if he was serious. He stood there watching me, no trace of a smile on his face. I cleared my throat. "What do you mean?"

Cliff shrugged and lowered his eyes. "They need it. We have thirty-four dollars, and they don't really have anything."

"That's not true," I said automatically.

Cliff took a deep breath and sighed. "I just think it might help them."

I started walking again, sneaking glances of Cliff out of the corner of my eye every few steps. This wasn't right. Cliff was the baby. The odd one. The kid who didn't care about anything but Jupiter and Spain and stacking his cans in rows.

So why did it suddenly feel like he was the grown-up and I was the child who needed chastising?

My blood pounded. "No. We aren't giving that money to Mama and Dad. We worked long and hard to earn it. *I* worked long and hard. I won't let it go wasted." My voice sounded hollow even to my own ears.

Cliff sighed again. "Whatever you say."

Feeling cold and lonely, I wrapped my arms around my chest. *Why should I feel lonely? I'm with Cliff and Grandpop Barley, right?* Or, actually, just Cliff, now that I looked around. I straightened. "Cliff, where's Grandpop Barley?"

He turned halfway and pointed. Standing at the end of Ima Nice's driveway was Grandpop Barley. He stood beside the mailbox staring at the house with a sad hunger in his eyes.

I hurried to his side. "What on earth are you doing?"

"Ima ..." Grandpop Barley turned to me, looking confused. "Is she...?"

I followed his gaze to the house. All the curtains were closed. No car sat in the driveway, and no lights shone softly from inside.

I scrunched my forehead. "I thought you knew that ..." I cleared my throat. "Grandpop Barley, Mrs. Nice passed away last week. Pastor Greene said she had a stroke and was sent to the hospital. She never made it home. The funeral was a couple days ago, but I don't think anyone really went."

Grandpop Barley's face crumpled like a paper ball. His body collapsed against the mailbox, and he began staring at the door in silence for what felt like hours. His face was unreadable—an eerie combination of pain and confusion. Finally, he turned to me. "There was a funeral?"

I swallowed past the prickly lump growing in my throat. "Yeah, but we missed it." Looping my arm in his, I drew him to his feet and away from the driveway. "Come on. We've got to go home now."

We followed Cliff back to our house, but none of us spoke a word. Instead, the silence hung over us. I could feel it in the air— a heavy blanket of sadness. Sadness for Juli, sadness for Grandpop, sadness for Mama and Dad …

I squeezed Grandpop Barley's arm, desperate for a way to make things better. "What do you think of an extra serving of peanut butter after supper, Grandpop? I'll bet I can talk Mama into it."

He didn't answer, staring blankly ahead at the road before us.

• • •

Grandpop Barley didn't eat any supper. His extra-large spoon of peanut butter remained untouched, along with his potatoes and bread and beans. He stared at his fork, his face scrunched in misery.

Mama and Dad didn't notice. Probably because they didn't eat either. They glanced at each other from time to time. Occasionally, one of them said something to me or Cliff. But for the most part, they just sighed and blinked back tears.

The sound of my clanging fork resonated through the dining room. After a few bites, I pushed my chair back and wiped my mouth. "May I please be excused?"

Mama nodded, half-heartedly motioning for me to take my plate to the kitchen. After clearing my plate, I led Grandpop Barley upstairs for his bath. He stared at the walls as he walked. Not blinking, not speaking. Barely even breathing.

Chills ran up my spine at the deathly calm look on his face. This wasn't Grandpop Barley. Not the one I knew, who argues and grunts and complains incessantly. "Grandpop Barley? Do you think—"

But I never got to finish my question. Because, in the blink of an eye, Grandpop Barley was falling toward the floor. He took down framed photos with him, flinging his hand across the wall. Glass shattered as each picture crashed to the ground. I could only scream and duck. The noise of breaking glass and Grandpop's deafening shouts rang in my ears.

When I opened my eyes, Grandpop Barley was writhing on the ground. His arms were outstretched like he was reaching for something he couldn't grab. "She's coming," he moaned. "I just know she's coming. She wouldn't leave me!" His breath shortened until he was gasping. "Not like this."

I jumped up and leaned against the railing. It let out a loud creak and I pulled away, shivering.

"Scarlett! Grandpop!"

I looked down and saw Mama and Dad standing at the bottom of the steps, looking horrified. Mama lunged toward me, but Dad held her back. "There's glass, Vida," he said, his voice harsh.

There was glass. Everywhere. Small shards were embedded in Grandpop Barley's face as he rolled around on the floor. Blood trickled down his pale white cheeks.

I pushed myself against the wall as Dad ran by me to kneel by Grandpop's side. My chest rose and fell, but it didn't feel like any air was getting in. I clenched my fists and immediately winced in pain. Unfolding my hand, I saw why: little bits of glass were stuck in my palm, glistening in the lamplight. My eyes squeezed shut. Never before had I felt so scared.

Scared that our family would shatter, like the glass frames. Scared that Grandpop would hurt himself, or one of us. Scared that things wouldn't be "okay" anymore.

I looked down and saw Cliff standing at the bottom of the steps, behind Mama. Tears welled up in his giant brown eyes. The same tears that were reflected in my own.

After he pulled all the glass out of Grandpop Barley's skin and helped him to his room, Dad stood at the top of the steps, his eyes lowered. "Vida, help your father wash his face." He glanced at me and Cliff. "Scarlett, let me see your hands." After he inspected them and cleaned out the glass, his gaze fell on the railing. "And stay away from that until I fix it. No need for anyone else to get hurt."

I didn't go to bed. At least not to sleep. I sat on my floor for over an hour, lost in the silence and darkness of my room. When I couldn't stand sitting there any longer, I pushed my door open and stood at the top of the steps. I could hear Mama and Dad's voices, drifting from their room. Mama was crying, and Dad was speaking softly.

My head pounded and I felt ill. *I have to make things okay. I have to do something.*

I ran to my room and grabbed the money jar from my night-stand. With trembling hands, I pulled out the thirty-four dollars and clenched it in my fist. Then I crept down the stairs and knocked on my parents' door.

Mama gulped before saying, "Come in."

I pushed the door open. "It's me."

"Come in, Scarlett," Dad said. His arms were wrapped around Mama's waist.

I stepped into the room, shutting the door behind me. My eyes darted around the bedroom. I hadn't been allowed in very often. The door was always shut. The room seemed big and empty, filled with laundry baskets and Dad's dirty overalls.

"Um, I …" My throat felt clogged and thick. I swallowed and held out the money. "Here. Cliff and I wanted to give this to you both. It'll help with something."

Dad shook his head. "No, Scarlett. We couldn't."

I placed the money on the dresser. It lay in a small pathetic heap. Not very much, but still probably more than Mama and Dad had in the bank.

"Just take it. Please."

I turned to leave.

"Scarlett?" Mama whispered. She pressed her lips together, tears in her eyes. "Thank you."

I nodded and left, heading back up the stairs.

Chapter 14

The next morning, Mama and Dad sat us down for a family talk. Without Grandpop Barley.

Cliff was the first one to notice. He sat on the edge of his seat, twitching his legs while his eyes darted back and forth across the room. "Where's Grandpop Barley?"

Mama took a deep breath. "That's what this discussion is about."

I chewed my lip and leaned back, pressing my fingers into the floral upholstery on the sofa.

Dad cleared his throat and glanced at Mama. "We think …" he sighed. "Grandpop Barley isn't himself anymore. He's been acting strange for a while, but lately it's just gotten … worse." He let out a deep breath. "We thought having him here would be okay, until last night. Then we realized that his mental sickness isn't just bad for him, it's putting you both in danger too."

I sat up. "Dad, we're fine. Neither of us is …"

"Scarlett." His voice was low and firm. "Show me your hand."

My insides felt like they'd sunk to the pit of my stomach. Slowly, I raised my hand. Small red cuts covered my palm.

Mama winced at the sight. "You see, honey? We just …" She glanced at Dad again. "We realized last night that we have no other choice."

Cliff licked his lips. "No other choice than what?" His voice sounded hoarse and tense.

"We're sending Grandpop to a home."

The words didn't sink in. *A home?* I blinked. "I don't understand. This is his home."

Dad shook his head. "I mean a new home. Someplace where he can be taken care of and watched. Somewhere he can't hurt himself or anyone else."

Numbness spread across my entire body. The kind of numbness where I couldn't think—couldn't speak. All I could do was stare at my parents. And wonder what kind of a cruel world I'd been placed in.

The sound of the doorbell jerked me out of my numbness. I stood, my body tingling. "I should get that." I walked toward the door, feeling as if I was living in some other universe, watching myself from the outside. *This can't really be happening, can it?*

I opened the door and found myself face-to-face with Frank Leggett. He was pacing the step, a frown tugging at his mouth. When he saw me he stopped and ran a hand through his hair. "I just heard."

I blinked. *That was fast. How did he …*

"Is she okay?" Frank's voice was etched with concern.

My brow puckered. "You mean *he*? I don't know. We're all kind of—"

"No," Frank said, cutting me off. "Juli. Do you know where she is? Has she contacted you?"

Juli? He'd come all the way over here to ask about Juli's disappearance when our whole family was falling to shreds?

I worked to keep my voice level. "She's with her boyfriend. I don't know where they went."

Frank shook his head, his face falling. "Your family must be going crazy. You must be sick with worry about her."

Um, no. Actually, we're sick with worry about the fact my grandfather nearly killed himself last night rolling around in broken glass.

I pressed my lips together and stepped onto the porch, closing the door behind me. "Is that the only reason you came over here? To ask about Juli?"

Frank blinked, looking confused. "Yeah."

I nodded. "Right. Okay, then." I turned away from him and put one hand on the knob.

"Wait."

My body tensed. I turned slowly. Frank was still standing on the top step, frowning at me.

"Are you okay, Scarlett? What has you so upset? Is it Juli?"

Plunge. Go ahead and plunge. I took a step forward. "Do you love Juli? Is that why you're always talking about her and staring at her with moony eyes? Because you're in love with her?"

"Um." Frank shifted, looking confused. "Well, I like Juli. I always have. You know that."

A cold wave swept over me, despite the ninety-degree weather. I wrapped my arms around my chest to keep from shivering. "Why?"

I knew it was rude to pester him. It was none of my business. And yet I had to know what it was that made Juli something to Frank that I could never be.

"Well …" He cleared his throat. "She's wild and beautiful and …" He gulped, refusing to meet my eyes. His voice faltered. "Well, she's …"

"She's what?" I whispered.

"She's perfect."

Perfect. The word bit into my skin, gnawing through my chest. And then, suddenly, all of the emotions that had been building in me for the past two days seemed too heavy to hold back anymore. I shook my head, aware of the cynicism growing in my heart.

"Perfect? You wouldn't know perfect if it bit you on the nose."

Frank reached out a hand toward me. "Scarlett, what's gotten into you? I don't understand."

I jerked back to avoid his touch. "Of course you don't understand!" I squeezed my arms tighter around my chest. "Juli isn't perfect, Frank. *We* are perfect. Perfect together." I shook my head, my voice dropping to a whisper. "You know, for such a smart kid, you are the stupidest boy I have ever met."

Then I turned one last time and slammed the door, leaving him alone on the porch. I couldn't bear that look on his face. The expression of confusion and embarrassment and ...

And what? I sighed and trudged back up to my room. *And why should I even care anymore?*

● ● ●

"Can I go with you?"

"I already told you no."

Cliff frowned and crossed his arms. He was standing in front of the door, blocking my exit from the house. "You never take me anywhere anymore."

"Don't be ridiculous. I took you on a walk the other day with Grandpop Barley. Remember?"

"Wasn't much of a walk," he muttered. But he moved aside and let me pass.

"Thanks." I glanced up at the sky. Dark gray clouds covered the sun, and the tops of the trees were swaying in the breeze that was picking up. Looked like a typical late-summer thunderstorm was sweeping through the state.

I'll be back before it starts raining anyway.

I hopped off the front porch and grabbed my bike. "I'm just going to visit with Mrs. Greene for a few minutes, okay, Cliff? If Mama asks where I am, tell her I'll be home soon."

He kicked at the doorframe, avoiding my eyes. "Scarlett never talks to Cliff anymore," he said, his voice soft. "She doesn't care about family."

Referring to himself in third person. He hasn't done that in forever. My leg hovered in the air, suspended halfway between climbing onto my bike and running over to shake some sense into Cliff. His words jabbed at my chest.

Oh, he's just doing it to get under my skin. I climbed all the way onto my bike and pushed up against the handlebars. "I can't handle this right now, Cliff. Just tell Mama, okay?"

Then I pushed off on the edge of my toes. Loose gravel slid under my sneakers. I pedaled hard and fast, away from the house and away from all the problems there.

The air had that weird dank smell that enveloped everything before it rained. It smelled like peaches rolled around in upturned soil.

I didn't even know why I had to talk to Mrs. Greene so badly. I had no idea why I thought that she would say something to make things better, or at least all right.

No cars were in her driveway when I pulled up. My bike skid to a stop at the edge of the front yard. *Is no one home? Should I even bother ringing the doorbell?*

Something fluttered at the curtain by the kitchen. I breathed a sigh of relief. *She's home.*

Ding-dong.

For someone with a relatively modest-sized home, the Greenes had quite a resounding doorbell. I could hear it echoing deep within the house. It practically made the door shake.

Mrs. Greene was smiling when she greeted me. Today, she was wearing a long floral dress with big red flowers, and had an apron tied around her waist. "Why, hello there, Scarlett! I thought I saw you from the window! How are you? Won't you come in?"

She led me inside and sat me down in the kitchen right up at the bar. It looked like she'd been baking recently. There was flour all over the counters, and the sink was piled up with dishes. One of her old cookbooks was lying open by the stove, but I was too far away to see what recipe she'd been trying out.

"Oh, here. You have got to try one of these." She leaned over and snatched a cookie off a china plate on the kitchen table. "I made them for the deacons' wives meeting this evening. They're lemon meringue *cookies*! Taste it, and tell me what you think."

I took a bite and wiped the crumbs off my face. "Delicious. I think you got the perfect combination of sweet and tart."

"I know!" She laughed and pulled off her apron. Grabbing a glass of iced tea, she settled onto the bar stool next to me and patted my arm. "So what brings you here today? Everything okay?"

Hardly. I racked my brain trying to think how to answer the question. "Um, yes and no."

"Sounds complicated."

"It is."

I explained to her everything that had happened in the last few days, from Juli leaving to Grandpop Barley falling to the embarrassing episode with Frank. Every horrible, awkward, painful detail was included.

"My parents have decided to send Grandpop Barley to a home in Savannah for mentally disabled people," I explained, rubbing at a spot on the counter. "It's about an hour away, which isn't far, but Cliff is just devastated."

"Why? Why Cliff and no one else?"

I blinked. "Well, I mean, we're all sad, of course, but it's for the best. You should have seen Grandpop the other night." Shivers ran up my back. "His face and hands were bleeding, and it was just … awful."

Mrs. Greene stood up and motioned toward the pitcher of iced tea on the kitchen table. "Would you like some?"

"Sure."

She walked over to her cabinet and pulled out a glass. Then she leaned against the counter. Her green eyes studied me carefully. "Let me ask you a question, Scarlett. If Grandpop Barley goes to this mental home, do you think that life will get better for you? For all of you?"

What kind of a question is that? I blew into my cheeks and puffed them out. "I don't know. I guess so. We won't have to worry about him getting hurt, at least."

Mrs. Greene filled the glass and handed it to me before sitting down again. "How does Cliff feel about it? You said he was devastated?"

"Yeah." I took a sip of the tea, and sucked on an ice cube that had slid with it. "Everything's just been so crazy lately. I guess I haven't had much attention to give him. It's just …" I sat up in my seat and leaned my elbows on the counter. "He doesn't seem to understand how life works. He has it in his head that we should all just work together and figure out a plan and it'll get better, but life just doesn't happen like that. Know what I mean?"

Mrs. Greene was quiet for a long time, sipping on her tea and staring at me in silence. I squirmed. Did I say something wrong? Mrs. Greene sighed and set down her glass. "I wish I could figure out something to tell you, Scarlett, but I don't think you'll like anything I have to say. It's like I told you, sometimes it takes more than just your own strength to find true peace and contentment. I'll certainly pray that by sending Grandpop Barley away, your family will be able to heal completely. But I just don't know if that will make things any better."

I stiffened. "Well, I should probably go."

Immediately, her face crumpled. "Oh, Scarlett! I've made you upset."

"No, no. You haven't." I wiped off my mouth and handed her my glass. "But it looks like it's about to storm, and I don't want to get caught in the middle of it on my bike."

Mrs. Greene's eyes looked doubtful, but she placed my cup in the sink and let me leave. "Be safe! And I'll be praying for you," she called as I ran down the front steps.

It was already starting to drizzle when I left her house. By the time I reached my driveway, I was stuck in a full-on rainstorm, with wind and stinging raindrops whipping at my face. My legs were aching from pedaling so hard, but I finally reached the end of the driveway. I dropped my bike and ran up the front steps. Cliff was still sitting by the door waiting for me.

My mind was whirling from my conversation with Mrs. Greene. *Was she right? Should I be fighting to keep Grandpop Barley here too?* I clenched my fists into little balls and then released them. Tight and loose. My heartbeat pounded through my wrists.

No, I just need to let it go. Anything for the sake of making things simpler around here. Cliff would be so much easier to handle without Grandpop Barley around, and I don't want to make things any more stressful for Mama and Dad. I couldn't bear to see that incident after Juli left played out all over again.

"Cliff's been waiting for Scarlett," Cliff said. He glared up at me with his brown eyes. His hair was sticking up off his forehead like he'd been running his hand through it all afternoon. "Scarlett needs to talk to Cliff."

I sighed. He was blocking the doorway again. "Cliff, just let me get through, okay? I have to fix something for supper."

"No. Scarlett needs to talk to Cliff *right now!*"

Okay, now this was starting to get on my nerves. The wind was howling all around us, and I could hardly hear myself think. Now was not the time for Cliff to be getting weird again.

"Cliff, please. Just move, okay?" The words were spoken through gritted teeth. My shirt was sticking to my skin; my hair was matted to the back of my neck.

He stood up and gave me a big shove. "No!" His chin was shaking. "Scarlett must listen to Cliff!"

His push sent me off balance, and I stumbled backward. I nearly fell down the front steps, but my hand caught hold of a porch pillar and I managed to regain my balance. Clinging to the wooden beam, I rubbed the hair out of my eyes and screamed, "Cliff! Just stop it! Stop talking like that! Can't you see I don't want to talk right now?"

We both fell silent. My words hung in the air between us. My chest was heaving up and down, and so was Cliff's.

Thunder boomed, and a few seconds later lightning lit up the sky.

Immediately, I regretted shouting at Cliff. It wasn't like me at all. I never yelled, never lost my cool. I sighed and stepped forward. "Look, Cliff, I'm sorry, I …"

Shaking his head, he yanked open the door and ran inside, banging it shut behind him. The sound of the door slamming into place rang in my ears. I reached forward to touch the knob and saw that my hand was trembling. *What's the matter with me?*

Turning around, I walked over to the edge of the porch and sat on the top step. *Deep, slow breaths, Scarlett. Healing breaths.*

The look on Cliff's face was ingrained in my head. That mixture of hurt, anger, and, worst of all, disappointment. Disappointment in me for not sticking up for him or for our family.

He just doesn't understand. I squared my shoulders. *Cliff always says that I don't need to be afraid of growing up. Well, this is it. This is growing up. Taking responsibility.*

Somehow, it didn't seem that way.

I'll just go inside and apologize to him after dinner. Read to him, if I have time. He'll be okay once we can distance him from Grandpop Barley's madness.

I stood and brushed off my soaking-wet jeans. *We'll all be okay.*

• • •

I folded Grandpop Barley's clothes neatly and placed them in his old leather suitcase. His initials were still engraved on the front: *GFB*. My fingers traced the letters before I closed the case with a slam and locked it.

I wondered if they'd have peanut butter at the home. If they allowed red ties and good bedtime stories.

Grandpop Barley never heard the ending to Peter and Wendy. For some reason, the thought pinched my heart. I sent up a silent prayer that the new home would have books about Peter Pan.

Old Clunker was running in the driveway. I could hear it all the way upstairs. As I started toward the truck, I noticed Cliff sat in the doorway of Grandpop Barley's room and stared down the steps with a sullen expression.

"Knock, knock," he said.

"Not now." I brushed past him, refusing to look at his red-faced tears. I'd already apologized to him a few days before, and we were good now. We didn't need another repeat of the crying and shouting incident.

"It's not fair," I heard him mutter. "Grandpop Barley's not crazy. He just misses Mrs. Nice. It makes him sad."

What does Cliff know about love? What does Cliff know about anything besides the Spanish Civil War? I pressed my lips together. "It's just not worth fighting, Cliff."

And it wasn't. Nothing felt worth fighting. I adjusted my grip on the suitcase. "Come on, Dad's waiting for us in the truck." I headed down the stairs, struggling under the weight of the luggage.

Dad honked the horn. "Kids!" he shouted.

My heart sank. Once I loaded that suitcase into the tailgate of the truck, it would be the last drive we'd ever take with Grandpop Barley. And after today, we wouldn't see him much at all.

Cliff ran to the edge of the staircase, leaning over the rail. His hair stuck up on his forehead, as if he'd been trying to pull it all out. "No! Cliff's not going! This is *family*. And family doesn't leave family."

I turned on the steps, sighing. *Really? More referring to yourself in third person?* "Come on, Cliff. You just don't understand." Cliff never understood when it came to dealing with people or situations. "Let's just go."

"No." Tears glittered in his swollen eyes. His face pinched a show of stubbornness. "We can't go with them. We can't let them do this, Scarlett. Grandpop Barley is part of our family."

I shook my head, unable to say what was replaying in my head: *But this isn't really much of a family anymore.* I looked away and reached the bottom of the steps. "Coming!" I called.

"Scarlett, don't!" Cliff shouted, leaning against the railing with one arm outstretched toward me.

What happened next is ingrained in my mind forever.

The first thing I heard was a horrible *crack*—the sound of breaking wood. A horrible rushing sounded inside my head, pounding along with my beating heart.

I froze, every muscle in my body tense. I wanted to turn around—I needed to turn around—but my body wouldn't move.

The truck door slammed. Dad took a step toward the house, squinting at me. His face looked tense. "Scarlett? What was that?"

Finally, I turned. Cliff was sprawled across the floor, splinters of wood lying around him. His head was turned at a strange angle. I stared at him. At his motionless body. At the broken railing.

And then, as if someone had sloshed a bucket of cold water over me, all the nerves in my body woke up in a deafening scream.

I was on the floor beside him in less than a second and rolled him over. His face and hands were covered in blood from his mouth. It trickled onto my jeans, staining them red. The faint thought crossed my mind that maybe he hit his chin on the banister. A few of his teeth looked chipped. "Cliff!" I shook him slightly. "He's not waking up," I muttered to myself. My voice rose. It sounded thick and clogged, like I was in a dream. "He's not moving. Dad, he's not moving!" I screamed.

Dad bounded into the doorway, clutching the frame with white knuckles. He swore out loud before collapsing on the floor and pushing me out of the way. "Don't touch him!"

My blood flashed between an unbearably hot tingle and a paralyzing freeze. The room seemed to twist and spin. My eyes worked like two little cameras, picking up all of the details around me.

The wood chips on Cliff's clothes. The jagged pieces of railing scattered across the hardwood floor. The blood smearing Cliff's unmoving head.

Shaking, I turned toward the doorway. Mama stood in the threshold, her face white. Her shoulders heaved up and down in labored breaths as she stared at Dad cradling Cliff's body. Wordlessly, her eyes moved across the room and met mine.

"He's still breathing," Dad said as he bent close to Cliff's face. "He's still alive. But he's not opening his eyes."

I attempted to speak, but no words came out. I glanced at Dad and tried to clear my throat. "What do we ...?" The words were scratchy and weak. "Dad, what do we do?"

Dad's tone was quiet and tense. He didn't look at me or Mama. "Call 9–1–1." Neither of us moved. His head snapped around, sudden anger contorting his face. He cursed and shouted again for us to call 9–1–1.

I sprung to my feet and ran to the kitchen where the phone was sitting on the counter by the refrigerator. My hands were shaking as I rang the number. *Oh, dear God, don't take him. Oh, please let him be okay. Oh, please don't—*

"Hello?"

"Please help us." I gripped the phone, my fingers turning white.

"What is your emergency?" The voice on the line was calm and clipped.

I fought back a wave of nausea. "My brother fell from the second-floor railing. He's still breathing, but he's not moving. I don't know if his brain is okay or if ..." I shook my head, even though she couldn't see me.

"Would you please give me your address and phone number?"

My address? Why can't I remember my address? I gulped and racked my brain. After a few seconds, the information came back to me and I managed to give it to the operator before she hung up, assuring me that an ambulance was on its way. I dropped the phone and ran back to the hallway. I could faintly hear the handset hitting the cabinet door as it swung back and forth on its cord.

Dad was still on the floor with Cliff in his lap. Mama was sitting in the doorway, her head buried in her arms, rocking back and forth and sobbing.

"Is he going to be okay?" My voice sounded like it was a million miles away.

Dad didn't answer. "Is the ambulance on its way?" he asked instead.

I nodded. My legs felt too weak to stand, so I collapsed on the floor.

"What's going on?" Grandpop Barley shouted from the truck. I heard the door slam, and he came running into the house with his eyes wide. "What's going on? What's the ruckus? Did something happen to the peanut butter?"

He froze in the doorway, his eyes falling on the scene before him. A confused look flashed across his face. "What did you do with it? Where's the peanut butter?"

I pressed my hand against my mouth to stop from crying out. My knees shaking, I got up and wrapped my arms around Grandpop Barley. He resisted at first, pulling away from my touch. But then he stiffened and let me keep my arms tight around him.

"It's okay, Scarlett," he said into my hair. "They'll bring it back. We'll get that peanut butter soon."

A siren sounded in the distance, on its way up our long driveway. I turned my face into Grandpop Barley's shoulder and began to cry.

● ● ●

I'd never been inside a hospital before.

Grandpop Barley sat next to me on a bench outside of Cliff's room. Mama and Dad were allowed inside, but the staff told us that there was a room limit and that the two of us had to stay out as long as the doctors were in there.

So we sat on the cold wooden bench and waited for someone to come tell us what was going on. Grandpop Barley was snacking on a banana that one of the nurses had given him out of her lunch box. He was also rubbing at the bandages on his hands that Dad had put on after the fall a few nights ago. I kept slapping at his fingers to keep him from pulling the dressings off.

The clock at the end of the hallway seemed to be moving at a snail's pace. We'd arrived here at quarter past five. Now it was almost seven, and my stomach was rumbling.

I buried my face in my hands. *Not that it matters. I feel too sick to eat.*

Cliff opened his eyes when they pulled him out of the ambulance. He looked right at me with those deep brown eyes and blinked. But he didn't see me. There was no recognition there. No pain or fear or excitement. Just emptiness.

I shuddered, tightly wrapping my arms around my chest. *God, please ...* I gulped. Did I really have any right to ask God for something? I never tried praying to him before, at least not like this, so wouldn't starting now be like cheating? All those years of sermons came flooding back, warning me how God feels about people who take him for granted.

I didn't care. *God, please keep Cliff alive. Please don't let him die. I need him to be all right. Please.*

The door to Cliff's room swung open, and Dad stepped out. Without saying a word, he scooped me up into his arms and gave me a big hug. My chest tightened. *Does this mean ... Is Cliff ...?*

"He's going to be okay," Dad said, his voice muffled in my hair.

I felt my whole body loosen until finally my knees gave out, buckling like a folding chair. I let my father hold me tightly and started to cry. *He's going to be okay. He's fine. He's going to survive.*

All the anxiousness started to drain from my head. I'd never felt such relief.

"Now, there's something I have to tell you." Dad pulled back slowly, guiding me back toward the bench. He knelt on the floor by me, holding on to my hand with a tight trip.

My stomach sank. "What?"

Grandpop Barley took one last bite of the banana and smiled. "I'm finished!" He attempted to hand it to Dad, who didn't pay any attention to him. "Hey!" His voice grew gruffer. "I said I'm finished. Take it!"

Dad shot him a quick glance before taking the banana peel and placing it on his lap. He reached out to grab my hand again, but I snatched my hands away and sat on them. The warm heat of my body sank into my skin. I could feel my pulse quickening in my wrists.

"What do you have to tell me?" I said again, my voice shaking.

Dad took a breath and let it out in a short huff. "Cliff's body is fine. It wasn't as bad as it looked. He's going to have a few cuts and bruises for a while, but the doctors said he should recover quickly without any problems."

"Then what's wrong?"

"It's his brain." Dad winced as he said the words, as if shielding himself from my sadness and my hurt. "He doesn't recognize us anymore. Doesn't remember anything about us. Whatever was … *wrong* with him is even more wrong now. Does that make sense?"

Sense? The words coming out of Dad's mouth were not registering in my ears. I shook my head slowly. It felt like it weighed a hundred pounds.

"I don't know how else to say this, Scarlett." He sounded frustrated now. I wondered if he was upset at me for not understanding or at himself for having to tell me everything. He leaned forward and placed a hand on my knee. "Your brother is never going to be the same Cliff we knew. He'll be alive. Breathing and walking and possibly even talking. But he won't ever be Cliff again. He'll be someone else."

I felt sick again, like a kid who had eaten one too many pieces of cake on her birthday. Only there was no buzz, no excitement, and it wasn't my birthday. It was the worst day of my life. God had kept Cliff alive, but he'd taken him from me. I'd lost my little brother.

● ● ●

Dad drove us home from the hospital that night in Old Clunker. I was glad to get away from the sympathetic smiles from the nurses and the clock ticking in my ears.

They'd let me go in to see Cliff before I left. He'd been lying in the hospital bed, bandages on his face from where he'd gotten cut from falling. He looked up as I came in the room but didn't smile. I'd told him hi, and he didn't say anything back. He didn't look happy to see me. He looked scared, if nothing else.

The doctors had confirmed what Dad told me: that Cliff didn't recognize any of us. He had no concept of family or friends or conversation. To him, I was just a stranger with crazy hair, saying gibberish that he neither understood nor cared about.

I scooted as close to the car window as I could and pressed my nose against the glass. Mama sat next to me, her hands shaking in her lap. Glancing out of the corner of my eye, I saw a fat tear roll down her cheek and fall on the edge of her black shirt, turning into a colorless puddle on the fabric.

I looked away, back out the window. We drove past the Leggetts' peach farm. The smell of ripe peaches no longer filled the air. Nothing drifted through the truck's open window but the smell of overturned soil and grass. All the peaches were picked. The farm was empty.

Mr. Leggett's pickup truck sat parked in their driveway. The bed was filled with suitcases and other luggage. *That's right. Frank's leaving for college. Today.*

I pushed down the liquid building in my throat. Frank had showed up at the hospital as soon as he found out about Cliff. He sat next to me for a few minutes and gave me a quick hug. Said he was sorry and he wished he could undo what had happened. And then he left. And that was it. He didn't say he'd write. Didn't promise to call.

It was like I'd never known him. Like all the memories of one wonderful summer—every day filled with just the three of us—had been magically erased and forgotten.

Cliff might forget. Frank might even forget. But I'll always remember. No matter how hard I try, all of the memories of this summer will stay trapped in my head.

Chapter 15

I'd never really thought about what happened to people after someone they loved died. I guess I'd thought that they cried for a day or two and then went back to normal. Isn't that what the rest of the world did?

Except our normal would never be normal, even if we did somehow recover that quickly. Cliff was very much alive. We went and visited him every day and tried to talk to him, but he never said a word back to us. He'd mutter to himself about people or places that we'd never heard of. Every now and then, he'd shout something at a nurse. Each visit was further proof the Cliff I'd loved was dead.

Cliff was worse off than Grandpop Barley now. After a week of dutiful visits, my parents decided that Cliff would take Grandpop Barley's place at the facility for the mentally ill, and Grandpop would have to come home and live with us again. It made more sense to put him in Cliff's room, where he'd be closer to us, but no one could step in there anymore. That door remained firmly shut.

We drove to the home one Saturday afternoon in late September, after Cliff had been there for about a month. It was a good hour's drive for us, but we had been coming every weekend we could— even if he often acted like we weren't even there.

Like always, Stacey, the blonde girl behind the reception desk, looked up and beamed when she saw us come in. She had the whitest teeth I'd ever seen outside of a dental commercial.

"Oh, hey there!" she said, giving us a little wave. "I was wondering when Cliff's family would get here. Just follow me and I'll take you up to see him. Though just so you're aware, I think he figured out that they're going to take him on a walk this afternoon, so he may be a little wound up."

She led us up the stairs to Cliff's room on the second floor. Another young man, named Albert, stayed in the same room as Cliff. He was about twenty-five years old and had some kind of mental condition that made him think we were all apparitions, so he was pretty freaked out most of the time. I tried to focus more on Cliff than Albert whenever we were there.

Stacey knocked on Cliff's door and beamed at us. "Cliff, there's someone here to see you."

Another nurse opened the door and motioned us in. Mama, Dad, Grandpop Barley, and I filled up a large chunk of the room once we were situated inside. Cliff was sitting on his bed in the corner, attempting to pull on a jacket. He was vibrating, practically shaking in excitement as he tugged at the sleeves. He grunted a few times and looked at the nurse with wild eyes.

For the first time, he seemed interested in something going on around him. *Maybe the therapy is working, maybe this hospital is a good thing … maybe he'll recover enough to be Cliff again.*

The nurse walked toward my brother. "Oh, let me help you with that."

Instinctively, I stepped forward at the same time as her, reaching out to help Cliff with his jacket. He blinked at me and jerked away. My skin froze.

The nurse smiled at me apologetically, then stepped forward and helped Cliff into his jacket, zipping it up for him. "There you go, bud."

Mama lifted a hand to her throat, pressing her lips together. "Why—" Her voice was raspy. She cleared her throat and tried again. "Why doesn't he ever respond to any of us, but he lets the nurses get near him?"

Stacey's eyes became soft as she leaned against the door. I noticed she had little laugh wrinkles around her mouth, but she couldn't have been older than thirty-five. "You're not familiar to him."

"Not familiar?" Mama's face crumpled.

Dad stepped forward and wrapped an arm around her shoulder. "He saw our faces every day for ten years. How could we not be familiar?"

The nurse who'd helped Cliff with his jacket folded her arms. "He doesn't have any memory of the last ten years. He doesn't have any memory of the last ten *hours*. Cliff operates on a minute-by-minute basis. By the time you leave today, he'll probably let you near him. He'll recognize you. But when you come again next week, he won't." She let out a little sigh. "If doctors could explain it or fix it, he wouldn't be here."

Mama gasped and pulled her thin cardigan close. She turned to Dad and muttered, "Well, that was an extremely rude thing to say. Very insensitive."

I watched the nurse closely to see if she cared. She didn't seem to. Instead of apologizing, she grabbed a baseball cap off of a hook on the wall and placed it on Cliff's head. "I'm sorry you folks can't stay longer today, but he's due for his daily exercise. Three loops around the building ought to do it. Stacey, will you hold the door?"

Stacey did as she was told and stood back as the nurse guided Cliff past us. "Say good-bye to your family, kid. They'll be back next week."

No one reached out to hug Cliff. Mama had tried that once and now had a small scar on her cheek from where Cliff had clawed at her. Instead, we all stood there mutely, watching a strange woman escort him away.

He brushed past me, his light denim jacket touching my skin. My heart stopped, and my stomach felt like it was in my throat. Then he looked at me and smiled. It was brief, but it was there, from the little curve of his mouth to the twinkle in his deep brown eyes.

I gasped. Everything in me lit up, spinning around at a hundred miles an hour and singing. And then he turned away and walked out the door, his face solemn again.

Still, it was there. He may not have recognized me, but he smiled at me. And that was something.

• • •

I'd imagined that the house would be different with Grandpop Barley gone, and had even braced myself for it. But nothing prepared me for what it felt like with Cliff missing.

Some days, I could handle it. I'd get home from school early, watch Mama leave for work, and sit upstairs with Grandpop Barley. Or I'd let him nap, and keep myself busy around the kitchen, baking and cleaning the counters until they shone.

But other times I'd wander the house like a ghost, once everyone was gone and Grandpop Barley was asleep. When I was alone, everything seemed to make me think of Cliff.

I sat on the couch and stared at the spot on the floor where Cliff used to sit and look at the pictures in his Spanish dictionary. His spot. I stood by the sink, my eyes fixed on the pile of cans waiting to be taken out to the trash. Those used to be Cliff's cans.

His spot. His chair. I was going crazy. I was pretty sure I'd read a book about someone who thought like that, and in the last few chapters, they'd ended up going crazy and jumping off a cliff. I wasn't sure if there were any high places like that in Georgia, but even just thinking about cliffs made me sad.

Maybe I was losing my sanity too. Maybe I would have a heart attack and die because Dad couldn't get me to the hospital fast enough in Old Clunker.

I wondered if death would be a good thing.

Dad's Bible was sitting on the coffee table next to the couch. I picked it up and flipped it open. The pages weren't worn at all; gold still glistened on the edges of the paper, undimmed by use.

Pastor Greene had announced he was preaching out of Psalm 25 on Sunday. Checking the table of contents, I flipped to the right page and started to read.

The words on the page tore at my chest: "Turn thee unto me, and have mercy upon me; for I am desolate and afflicted. The troubles of my heart are enlarged: O bring thou me out of my distresses."

I felt the affliction. I felt the distress. Cliff was alive, but it wasn't good enough. Grandpop Barley was home and fairly happy, but it didn't make me feel any better. Because my life still felt shattered and broken and empty.

My eyes slid shut, tears pulling at the corners. *Why won't the pain go away? Why does it hurt so much for me, God? Why can't you take away the hurt and the sadness?*

I closed the Bible and left my hand on the cover, feeling the cool leather beneath my fingertips. I couldn't understand how everything had turned so black. I ached to know—to know the answers. To understand what God was saying and to hear from him directly why this had to happen.

I thought about what Mrs. Greene had said a few days before Cliff's accident. *Sometimes it takes more than just your own strength to find true peace and contentment.* I knew what she'd meant. She'd wanted me to trust in God's strength.

Wrapping my arms across my chest, I glanced out the window.

Nearly bare trees lined the driveway, leading to the road; no cars or people were in sight. I wished I could see Cliff come running back down the driveway. Or maybe Juli. It was hard to separate it all in my head anymore.

● ● ●

I woke up the next morning before the sun had risen and wandered to Grandpop Barley's room. I pushed open the door and stood in the threshold, peering into the darkness. His large, bumpy figure curled into a tight ball filled the bed.

Closing the door gently behind me, I crossed the bedroom and sat by his bed. The last few moonbeams of the night cast their shadows across the hardwood floor at my feet, turning my skin an eerie white.

I sat silently, watching Grandpop Barley's chest rise and fall in sleep. His face looked so peaceful. The faithful red necktie lie loosely tightened on his neck and the sheets were clutched in his gnarly hands.

The sun slowly rose in the window behind me, illuminating the room in rosy pink sunlight. I watched the shadows moving across the floor as the hours passed. Every time I got up to leave, I felt something tug me back to the floor. I didn't know what it was, but there was something in that room that made me feel at least a little bit better.

Maybe it was the look on Grandpop Barley's face. That slight smile that made me wonder what he was dreaming about. Where he was, which was so much more wonderful than this house and all its bad memories. Maybe in his dreams he was flying above Neverland or eating giant jars of peanut butter without getting any on his fingers. He hated having sticky fingers.

I rested my chin in my hand and imagined Cliff sitting on the floor beside me making quips about how Grandpop Barley's face looks like some kind of gnarled Spanish tree. Or asking to turn on the television and see what was going on with the rockets and astronauts. Suddenly, the room seemed too quiet and too still. I climbed to my feet and gently shook Grandpop Barley.

"Time to wake up, Grandpop Barley. It's morning." Well, technically, it was probably closer to noon by now. But I need him to wake up. To hear him grumble and complain and know that things might almost be back to normal.

His eyelashes fluttered and opened, and he frowned at me. "Whaddya want? Can't you see I'm busy?"

I shook my head and waved a hand nonchalantly. "Never mind. Go back to sleep."

I left his room, closing the door behind me. I rushed across the hallway and into my room and pulled off my pajamas. Opening my dresser, I yanked out my oldest pair of jeans and a faded shirt. I had to get away.

● ● ●

The air outside smelled sugary and fresh. The last gasps of the hot Georgia summer were still kicking well into October, providing warmer temperatures and little breeze. I walked in sandals down the dirt road, kicking at little rocks in my path.

I stopped in front of Mrs. Ima Nice's house. Pastor Greene's pickup truck was parked out front. He stood by the front door with a large board in his hands. Not noticing me, he lifted the board and laid it across the door, hammering it into place.

"Hey!" I shouted without thinking. "What do you think you're doing?"

He jumped and whipped around. "Scarlett?" His eyes squinted, and he took a step forward, like he thought I wasn't truly there. "Scarlett Blaine?"

I crossed my arms and stomped up to the house. "You can't just board up her doors. It's not your property."

Pastor Greene lowered the wood and nails. "The bank is closing up the house. It's going to be demolished next spring to make way for a new grocery store. They figured it would be better for the community than to leave it vacant."

"But ..." Tears stung at my eyes. I looked around at the empty porch. "But this is where Mrs. Nice used to sit in her rocking chairs and yell at us. There were two of them." My voice cracked. "Right here." I pointed.

Pastor Greene scratched the back of his neck, looking uncomfortable. "Look, Scarlett, I know this is a very difficult time for you right now, but you have to understand. This is all for the best. If the house stays vacant, it will eventually become rundown and rickety. The paint will chip, and the bushes will become overgrown. Local teenagers will come here to throw rocks through the windows and do stupid stuff."

I stared at the house that was no longer a home while he talked, my mind whirling. Just two months ago, it was all so different. I never knew—never imagined—that any of this could have happened. Everything had been so wonderful.

Pastor Greene picked up the board again, watching me to see if I'd stop him. "Mrs. Nice was very proud of her home, remember? She would turn over in her grave if she knew it had become a laughingstock of the community."

My eye caught sight of something. A medium-sized cardboard box labeled *For Church Sale*. Photo frames and bits of clothing peeked out from over the side. I imagined the old ladies at church rummaging through her boxes and gossiping about her belongings. My temper flared. "You are not going to sell her things at a church sale!" Without thinking, I snatched the box off of the porch steps and ran, not looking back.

"Scarlett!" Pastor Greene shouted behind me. "Scarlett!"

It was a pretty good-sized box, and I was pretty winded not long after I left the porch. He could have caught me if he wanted. I don't even think he tried. Maybe it was meant to belong to me all along.

I ran until I reached our driveway. Then I collapsed on the ground by the mailbox and set the carton down next to me. A pile of framed photos lay on top, a little jumbled from the ride. I pulled them out one by one. There were photos of Ima Nice as a child, a bride, a mother, and an older woman.

Nestled underneath all of the photos was an unframed photo of Ima Nice and Grandpop Barley taken about fifty years ago. Photographs must have been pretty new back then. The picture was grainy and blurry, but I recognized him by the curve of his smile and the dent in his chin.

They were standing under the shade of an apple tree. In all of the other photos, Ima had been wearing fancy church frocks and hats. In this one, she was in a simple cotton dress, her dark hair falling around her shoulders. He wore thin trousers and a rumpled shirt, his arm slung around her shoulder. Both were smiling.

I wrapped my fingers around the photo and slid it into my pocket. Then I piled the rest back into the box and carried it into the house, plopping it down in the garage. *Well, it may not belong to Ima Nice anymore, but at least there won't be any snoopy old gossips digging through her things.*

The picture I saved until later, when I was alone. I smoothed out the edges and placed it in a frame, switching out a picture of me smiling with missing teeth. Then I carried it up the stairs and placed it by Grandpop Barley's bedside. *There. Now it'll be the first thing he sees when he opens his eyes.*

I looked at the smiling man in the photo one last time before dropping my gaze to the sleeping one in front of me. "I just want everyone to be happy again," I whispered, lightly touching Grandpop Barley's forehead, then leaving.

Chapter 16

It was the first Saturday in December, which meant visiting day at Cliff's facility. We all piled into Old Clunker and headed toward the city. A few houses were starting to put wreaths out on the front doors. It felt like a nice, cheery start to the holiday season.

Mama wrapped her arms around her chest and glanced at Dad from the passenger seat. "I don't want any Christmas decorations this year. I just want everything to keep going on normally so we can forget about how we're supposed to feel this month."

That idea didn't upset me as much as I thought it would. The last thing I wanted to do was wake up Christmas morning and stare at a fat tree with no presents and no siblings beside it.

The home didn't get the memo about the no-Christmas thing, though. They were already in full-on holiday mode; a Perry Como carol greeted us as we walked into the lobby.

Mama grimaced and grabbed Dad's hand. We said our hellos to Stacey and headed upstairs to visit with Cliff. Today, they had him dressed in a lightweight reindeer sweater. His small room was covered in candy canes, and Albert sat in the corner looking over some Christmas cards his family must have sent him. I'd overheard someone say they lived in Alabama and sent him here so he'd get better medical attention.

Cliff was sucking on a candy cane when we walked in. He held it up to show us, a big smile on his face. I guess if he was sugared up enough, he was too happy to be shy.

"Well, hello there, Cliff!" Dad, obviously encouraged by the smile, took a step forward.

Bad idea. Cliff's happy expression immediately fell away, and he crawled back into his bed, refusing to look at us.

As a result we ended up standing by the foot of his bed for most of the visit and talking to him without being able to see his face. Mama told him about the Christmas potluck supper at church. Dad said a few things about getting the truck fixed (which wouldn't have interested Cliff anyway, but it's not like Dad knew that), and Grand-pop Barley asked for a candy cane. A nurse gave him one, and he sucked on it in silence.

I went last. I told Cliff that I was going to try to make Spanish quesadillas for dinner this week, and that I'd gotten an A on my last biology test, and that my teachers seemed to think I could go to any college I wanted to next fall. I also mentioned that there was talk of another space mission and that I was praying they'd pick Jupiter. He stiffened at that word but didn't make any move to look at me or say anything.

"Yeah, I guess that wouldn't be spectacular anyway," I said, crossing my arms. "You're going to be the first astronaut on Jupiter. Not some lousy NASA guy."

Cliff said something, but his voice was muffled by the sheets. I jumped forward. "What did he say? Cliff, what did you say?"

Stacey grabbed my arm and pulled me backward, away from the bed. "Don't get too close to him," she warned.

"But he said something," Mama protested. "We all heard him. He said something. What did he say?"

"*Sí*," I murmured.

Everyone looked at me. Stacey blinked. "What?"

"He said *sí*." It's a Spanish word." I looked back at him, buried under a mound of sterile white sheets and gray flannel blankets. "I know he said it." He remembered.

• • •

"Scarlett, can you help me with this?" Mama's voice sounded through the house.

I glanced at Grandpop Barley one last time to make sure he was asleep before climbing to my feet and making my way downstairs.

Mama was standing on the front porch, straining under the weight of a tall evergreen. "Help me with this, would you? It's really heavy."

I stopped in the doorway. "A Christmas tree? Seriously?" I felt as if someone had punched me in the gut. *I thought she said no memories. No reminders.*

"That old couple in the house next to the church donated it to us," Mama said, pushing a branch out of her face. "Your father picked it up at Pastor Greene's house this afternoon."

My face felt hot. "Why do they feel like they need to give us a tree? We didn't ask for one. We don't even have any of the decorations down or anything, and I thought we weren't planning on—"

"Scarlett." Mama stopped and turned to look at me. The tree was twisted in her arms, halfway in the door, the bottom half trailing down the steps. "Please." Her voice was whisper soft.

I looked up and caught her eye. The pain I saw there was evident. She wasn't any more joyful this Christmas than I was.

Pulling on a light sweater, I scurried out onto the porch and helped her drag the tree into the house. I strained under the weight. Pine boughs pressed into my skin and scratched my cheek. The spicy scent of sap filled my nostrils.

We set up the tree in the living room and stood back. It seemed so big and pretentious in the small empty space. Unadorned, it was just a big sweet-smelling hunk of greenery and sap.

I stuck my hands in my pockets and looked around. No other decorations were in sight. "Mama, do you want me to get the ornaments down from the attic?"

She gulped, pressing a hand to her throat. Tears glistened in her eyes as she stared at the Christmas tree. "No," she said, her voice sounding clogged. She cleared her throat and turned away. "No, I think it looks fine. I'm going to … I'll be in the kitchen."

I stared at the tree in silence. *It really is ugly. Ugly and stupid.* I kicked at the carpet and walked back upstairs, taking two steps at a time.

Grandpop Barley's door was shut. I knocked on it, but there was no answer. Pushing the door open, I tried to smile brightly. "Grandpop Barley! Guess what we got!"

I blinked, my eyes adjusting to the dimness. They fell on the bed, where he lay curled up in a small ball. My heart sank like a lead weight. *Oh, Grandpop Barley.*

I perched on the edge of the bed and gently touched his leg. "We got a Christmas tree downstairs. Do you want to see it?"

He grumbled a bit and rustled under the sheets. His head remained buried in the pillow, turned away from me. And he wasn't wearing his necktie anymore.

I reached out and gently touched his back. A million thoughts rushed through my mind, but the strongest gnawed at my stomach. *We should have never tried to send you away. Never.*

● ● ●

The unusually cool winter air pinched at my reddened cheeks. I wrapped my jacket tighter around me, snuggling into the warmth.

The air had that distinct Christmas aroma: a mixture of pine boughs and freshly mowed lawns. *I guess everyone in Georgia has a Christmas tree by now.*

I wandered through the streets with my hands in my pockets. Avoiding the glances of housewives through windows, I kept my eyes on the ground. Dead leaves crunched under every step.

I paused in the middle of the road and took a deep breath. *This is the spot where I rescued that turtle.* The skid marks of my bike had faded, of course, and a fresh layer of dirt covered the ground. My eyes drifted toward the pond. Smooth ripples moved across the surface of the water as the wind blew.

The soft rushing of wind filled my ears and tickled my cheek. I stood on the edge of the water and took a deep breath as I lifted my head to the sky. Thick, dense clouds covered the sun.

Everything was quiet. Too quiet. I was conscious of the heart pounding in my chest, of the breaths escaping my lips, of the hands clenching in my pockets. Conscious of the fact that, like it or not, I was still alive.

I'm still alive, and I must go on living. The thought filled me with a sickening discomfort. The thought of living … of going on like nothing had ever happened even though it had … I would never be the same because of it.

Juli's words floated through my subconscious. *"I think there's a divine happiness out there that brings about peace to the open mind."*

My throat burned. *God, my mind is open.* I stared back up at the sky, filling with bubbling anger. "Wide open!" I shouted. "And I'm not feeling anything!"

Ducks scattered around the pond, startled at my outburst. I pulled my arms back toward my chest, hugging myself tightly. I felt something hot and wet slide down my face, and realized I was crying. *Oh, God, I want to feel something.*

I sniffed. The moisture on my face was inviting a cold wind. I rubbed my nose.

Go to Mrs. Greene's house.

The thought came unbidden. Mrs. Greene? *I haven't been to see her in months. It'll only be awkward after everything that's happened ...*

My feet began to move, one step after another. I was walking toward her house, still uncertain as to whether I wanted to go.

What if she ... What if she talks about Cliff? What if she wants to know what happened with Frank?

And then I was standing at her little red mailbox, staring up at her house. It looked exactly the same, with the exception of a few dead flowers no longer blooming on the front porch.

Mrs. Greene is your friend. She would never make you talk about something you were uncomfortable with. She knows you.

I knocked weakly on the front door and stood back, my thoughts in a flurry. I rubbed my frozen hands together. *Maybe she didn't hear me. Maybe she's out and won't be back until ...*

The door opened, and Mrs. Greene stuck her head out. She blinked when she saw me, her eyes widening into two small full moons. "Scarlett, what a surprise! Come in."

She held open the door and stood back, letting me pass. I shivered and slipped out of my heavy jacket. "Here, I'll take that." Mrs. Greene hung the coat on a rack in the closet and led me to the kitchen. "It certainly is cold outside. Would you like a cup of hot tea?"

I nodded. "Thank you."

Mrs. Greene stood with her back to me as she began brewing a pot for us. "I must say it is a surprise to see you today, although I am pleased. I was wondering if you'd want to start up cooking lessons again. Tim was just saying he'd love you to teach me a few new recipes."

"No," I murmured. "I didn't come here for that."

"Oh. So then, what have you been up to?"

I shrugged, even though she couldn't see me. "Nothing."

"Here you go." She turned and handed me a steaming hot cup.

"Thanks," I said, pressing the tea to my lips and letting the warmth sweep through me.

"You know, this is the second time you've just shown up at my house, and I have a feeling it wasn't just because you were passing by." Mrs. Greene settled next to me and gently squeezed my arm. "How are you, Scarlett?"

I opened my mouth to respond with "Just fine" when it struck me that I wasn't fine. I wasn't even close to fine. I was broken and bruised and lonely. Every waking second I asked myself why: *Why are my family and I living like this? What's the point anymore?*

I took a heavy breath and set down my cup. "I came here because I need you to give me a reason to keep living, Mrs. Greene. No one's ever home. Cliff's gone and Grandpop Barley's ... quiet ... and I feel all alone. I need help. I don't understand ..." I cleared my throat, fighting back tears. "I just don't know what to do anymore."

Mrs. Greene's eyes flickered down to the table. She took one of my hands and folded it in hers, rubbing it gently. "What is it you want, Scarlett? What do you desire more than anything else in life?"

My chest squeezed. "I don't know! I want ..." I took a deep breath, looking around the kitchen, tears blinding my vision. *What do I want? I want Cliff to remember me. I want my family to be whole. I want Juli to come home. I want Frank to love me. I want for everything to be okay. I want ...*

"No." I shook my head, raising my eyes to Mrs. Greene's face. Pain was etched in it—pain that I knew reflected my own suffering and loss. I took a shaky breath. "The one thing I want more than anything is to have *peace*. I want to know that there's a reason for all this. So much has happened that can't be erased, but more than wanting to erase it, I just want to know that I'll be okay in spite of it. If I could just know that ..." I trailed off.

Mrs. Greene was watching me closely. She didn't say anything; she just waited for me to continue.

Shaking my head, I tried to explain the heaviness inside my chest. "There's so much more I could have done. I could have stopped Juli if I'd just been honest enough with her. If I'd just tried to talk to her and find out what was wrong. And I should have been there more for Cliff. Given him more things to remember. And I should have been there for Grandpop Barley. I let him down, and if I'd stood up for him, maybe then Cliff wouldn't have …" I bit my lip and willed the tears back. "It was my responsibility to keep the family together, and I just … I just couldn't do it well enough." My voice grew thick. "It just wasn't enough."

My words sounded empty and hollow. It was just like she'd said several months ago. My own strength just wasn't enough to find what I craved.

"Scarlett." Mrs. Greene reached out and squeezed my hand in her own. "No one could have a bigger heart than you. There's nothing else you could have done." Her eyes looked sad, and she rubbed my fingers softly.

I swallowed, forcing down the lump in my throat. "I can't go on without knowing that God is in control of this. Of my life. I need to know that no matter what happens, there is a reason for it all." My eyes were starting to water up, so I concentrated on staring at a small spot on the ceiling. My mouth was moving faster than my brain. I took a deep breath. "If I could just trust that God had a reason for it all."

Mrs. Greene nodded and stood, reaching for a Bible on the counter. She laid it on the table and flipped through the pages, her eyes skimming the text. Then she looked up at me. Reaching over to smooth a stray hair off my forehead, she gave me a small smile. "God always has a reason, Scarlett." She glanced down at the Bible.

"Here's a familiar passage, but I think it might be helpful to you.

Jeremiah 29:11–13: *"For I know the things I think toward you sayeth the Lord, thoughts of peace, and not of evil, to give you an expected end. Then shall ye call upon me, and ye shall go and pray unto me, and I will harken unto you. And ye shall seek me, and find me, when ye shall search for me with all your heart."*

Mrs. Green closed the Bible and looked at me. Her green eyes were bright and piercing. "God always has a plan, Scarlett. And if you are his child, then he promises that it will be for good. You may not know it right away. It may take years of pain and suffering to finally be able to look back and see how God was using trials in your life for good."

My chest pinched in confusion and frustration and bitterness. "Then I don't see the point. Why trust God if nothing will be any better?"

"Because"—Mrs. Greene pressed my hand gently—"you will never be without peace. You will never get to a point where your strength is gone and you don't think you can go on. God will always be there to protect you. Even when everything seems dark and there doesn't seem to be a light at the end of the tunnel, God will be there."

My lips felt dry. I chewed one corner and tried to calm my shaky chest. "How can I know that he's near?"

A soft smile spread on Mrs. Greene's face. "What did the Bible say?" She glanced down at the text and read it slowly. "And ye shall seek me, and find me, when ye shall search for me with all your heart." She looked up at me. Silence filled the kitchen, pierced by the unhindered ticking of the clock on the wall. Finally, she pressed her lips together and smiled. "It's up to you, Scarlett. Do you want to find him?"

I gulped, unable to find the words to express what I was thinking. My heart was pounding. Deep down, I knew this was what I wanted. To find God. To give over control of my life and trust him to take care of me.

Mrs. Greene pushed away from the table and grabbed the tea pot. "More tea?" But before she poured a drop, she hesitated. Pointing to my cup, she said, "You, just like your cup, are empty. There is nothing good in you. Nothing to fill you but God." She motioned toward the teapot. "Who knew tea could be so meaningful, right?"

I wanted to laugh, but my throat burned with the stinging tears I was holding back. I pressed my lips together and stared at the steam rising from my cup. "I don't ..." My voice broke to a whisper. "I don't deserve it."

"Scarlett, honey, it doesn't matter."

Involuntarily, my shoulders slumped and I buried my face on the table, erupting in tears. I cried without making a single noise, my chest aching for all the things I thought I'd done wrong and all the ways I could have made them right. If I'd only turned to God, instead of trying to do it all on my own.

God, forgive me. I'd wanted to say the words aloud, but even as I thought them in my head, I knew that it was enough. *Forgive me, and make me whole.*

Mrs. Greene rubbed my back in small circular motions. After my eyes were swollen beyond the point of seeing, I lifted my head and smiled. "Thank you," I whispered.

● ● ●

I was sitting in the kitchen when Mama came in. Pulling off her uniform gloves, she shut the door behind her and glanced at me. "Oh, I see you're already eating. Good. I think your dad will be working late tonight. He's doing that double-shift at the paper factory until peach season comes again." She shook her head. "And you won't believe how busy we've been at the bed and breakfast. Everyone wants a plantation-style Christmas getaway all of a sudden."

I took another bite of my sandwich and wiped the crumbs off my skirt. "Do they have a Christmas tree?"

Mama nodded and pumped some lotion onto her hands. "It must be ten feet tall." She smoothed the lotion into her skin, and I watched it dissolve in small swirls.

"You know"—I gulped down my food—"I'm thinking about decorating our tree tonight."

Mama blinked and froze. "Are you …?" She opened and closed her mouth but seemed unable to finish the thought.

I nodded. "I'm sure."

She rubbed the back of her neck and heaved a shaky breath. "I'll help you."

I made Mama a sandwich and sat with her at the table until she was finished. Then I carried the dishes into the kitchen and placed them in the sink. "I'm going to get Grandpop Barley. He might like to watch."

Grandpop Barley's room was dark as always. I switched on his light and knelt at the side of his bed. "Grandpop Barley," I whispered, shaking him gently. "Come downstairs. I want you to see something."

I helped him out of bed and into his robe. Then I led him down the stairs and settled him on the couch. "There. Now just sit and watch us decorate the tree."

Mama walked into the living room, struggling under the weight of several boxes. "I grabbed these out of the attic. I think they're all marked. Ornaments are in … this one." She held up the largest of the boxes. Kneeling on the ground, she opened the box and pulled out the first ornament. It was a gold-painted pinecone with *Juli, 1956* written on the side. Her shoulders slumped.

My heart pinched. *This is going to be harder than I thought.* Gently, I reached out and squeezed her hand. She looked up and smiled.

"Right. Now I think this one should go over here, don't you?"

I nodded and hung it on the far side of the tree, near the top. I stood back to admire the single ornament. "It looks good."

We spent the rest of the evening hanging the old ornaments one by one until the tree was filled.

"There," Mama said, standing back to appraise the last one. "What do you think?"

I settled on the couch next to Grandpop Barley and motioned for Mama to sit next to me. I soaked in the sight of the Christmas tree, heavy with our family's memories. A smile tugged at my lips. "It's beautiful."

Mama nodded, resting a hand over her mouth. Tears glistened in her eyes. "It looks ..." She sighed. "It looks like family."

I covered her hand with my own. "We're still a family," I whispered, lacing her fingers through mine.

She gulped and turned toward me, smiling. "You do know how much I love you, Scarlett?"

I hugged her in response. She smelled sweet, like the bread they baked at the bed and breakfast. Her hair was soft and warm against my cheek. I pulled back and rubbed her shoulders, feeling how thin they had become. "I love you too."

And I did. She hadn't been the best mother in the world. She was far from perfect. She'd taken me for granted before and ignored Cliff. She didn't know me inside and out—and probably didn't care to—but she did love me. And, in the end, I loved her too. That was all that really mattered.

"O, Christmas tree, O, Christmas tree, how lovely are your branches."

I jerked back and whipped my head around, shocked at the sound of Grandpop Barley's raspy voice. He was sitting with his hands in his lap, smiling contentedly at the pretty tree. He looked at me and gave a small smile.

I looked at Mama. She was beaming, her face sunny again.

The door in the kitchen opened, and I could hear Dad come in, dropping his keys on the counter. I jumped up. "Dad! Dad!"

His head popped around the corner, looking surprised. "What? What?"

"Grandpop Barley was just singing 'O, Christmas Tree,' at least one line. But the point is, he talked about something other than peanut butter!"

A grin spread across Dad's face. "Good." He glanced at the tree as he bent to kiss Mama. "It's beautiful, honey. Absolutely beautiful."

Chapter 17

"Well ..." Dad rubbed his hands together and attempted to break the silence filling the kitchen. Mama and I sat next to him at the table, eating with our eyes glued to our plates. "There's a political meeting in town tonight. I guess I'll take Old Clunker. Do either of you want to go?"

Mama glanced up, giving him a small smile. "Of course, dear."

I shrugged. "No, thanks." Taking another bite of chicken, I tried not to look at all the empty settings on the table. Cliff's. Juli's. And even though he was upstairs sleeping, Grandpop Barley's.

Deep breaths, Scarlett. We are still a family with or without them.

Pressing my napkin to my mouth, I slid away from the table. "May I please be excused? I have some homework to get done."

Dad looked up. "Are you sure you don't want to go with us tonight? You don't want to be all alone, do you?"

The words hit me like a bucket of ice water. *All alone.* My face strained. *I'm all alone all the time. Whenever you're both at work, I'm here by myself.*

Immediately, Dad reddened. "I didn't mean ... I only meant to say that ..."

"It's okay." I forced a smile. "Grandpop Barley's sleeping upstairs, right?"

Mama and Dad lowered their eyes, glancing at each other. I saw

Mama's hand slip off of her lap and squeeze his. The small gesture made my heart warm, for some reason. A reminder that we were still there for each other. That we would make it through this life together, somehow. I looked away and carried my plate to the sink.

I stood by the sink for a while and looked out the window. The sun was starting to set. I could hear Mama and Dad leave the table and head to their bedroom to grab their coats and shoes.

Turning off the water in the sink, I leaned against the counter and pressed my nose up against the window pane. It was slightly cool, wetting my skin. I closed my eyes and breathed in.

Give me a purpose, God. Give me something—anything—to take my mind off this pain and serve you instead.

I stood by the window and watched until I saw Old Clunker rev up and drive away in a cloud of dust. Then I tromped up the stairs and settled on the floor in my room. The house felt big and empty, even though I knew Grandpop Barley was asleep just down the hall. Somehow, it still felt like I was alone.

Well, I guess I'd better get started on that paper. I pulled my schoolbook out of my day bag and opened it up on the floor. Spreading out, I cracked it open and perused the title suggestions. *Five thousand words on the balance of power in the US government. Fun.*

Pulling my bag open, I searched for a pencil. *That's weird. I could have sworn there was one in here.* I dumped open the bag, pouring out the contents on the floor. Crumpled-up paper, candy wrappers, and loose change, but no pencil.

I bet there's one in Cliff's room. I stood and headed into the hallway, only pausing for a moment before pushing open Cliff's door.

The moment I did, my chest felt as if it had been hit by a wall of bricks. I hadn't been in his room since the day of his fall, but nothing had changed. Dirty clothes were still folded neatly on the floor, books were perfectly lined up on the shelves, and rows of blocks remained stacked along the wall. His battered copy of *The Complete Spanish Dictionary* was sitting on the edge of the bed.

Salty bile bubbled up in my throat. *Oh.* Tears pricked my eyes, stinging them to the point of blindness. I stood stock still and stared at all of Cliff's things.

The room seemed untouched by time. In this room, I could almost believe that Cliff was still here with us, laughing and talking. That he was upstairs firing up Grandpop Barley or downstairs stacking cans in the kitchen. After supper, we would ride our bikes to Frank's orchard and stare at the clouds and laugh until our sides hurt and we were too sleepy to keep our eyes open. And then I would watch Cliff crawl into bed and read him a chapter out of one of his favorite books, caving when he asked for one more because it was so adorable when he said, *"Por favor?"*

I just need to get a pencil and get out. I began rummaging through his drawers. *Get out before …*

My eyes fell on a book sitting on Cliff's dresser: *Peter and Wendy.* My chest tightened. I reached out and picked up the book, flipping through the pages. Illustrations of laughing Peter, worried Peter, surprised Peter, and triumphant Peter flashed before my eyes. In the back of the book was a folded piece of paper.

With trembling hands, I opened the paper and smoothed out the wrinkles. *My Birthday List. By Cliff Blaine. June 6, 1969.*

I scanned the list, remembering the look on Cliff's face as he read each of the items to me. *One monkey from Japan. Eight moons in the sky instead of one. Fifteen Spanish battles.*

And there it was, right at the bottom. *Sixteen rockets to Jupiter.* Written in his childish scrawl, smeared with frosting and smelling of peppermints.

As I stared at the piece of paper, the memories rushing over me stronger than a freight train, one thought echoed in my mind.

Cliff never got his rocket to Jupiter.

My legs folded beneath me. How could I have been so stupid? In the middle of Juli, and politics, and Grandpop Barley, I had forgotten the one who was the most precious to me. The little brother who had stuck by me and made me smile on horrible days and whispered that he wished he had ocean eyes like mine while he twirled his fingers in my tangled hair. Cliff, who had wanted that rocket more than anything in this world, but had given it up for the sake of our family's happiness.

My stomach twisted at the memory of our betrayal of that sacrifice. The day our family was hanging by threads, Cliff was the only one who cared about gluing it back together.

We can glue it together now. It's been ripped and shattered and scarred, but the pieces are still there. Just because Cliff had a bruised brain and Grandpop Barley couldn't remember his left from his right didn't make them any less family.

I looked back down at *Peter and Wendy*. Hidden in the back was another folded paper. When I pulled it out and opened it, a smile pulled at my lips.

It was a drawing of one giant spaceship, painted green, with the words *To Jupiter* sprawled across the front. An entire crew was drawn inside. Cliff, me, Frank, and Grandpop Barley with a vibrant red tie. We were smiling and waving as we hurtled into space.

Turning the page over, I saw a short message scribbled on the back:

Cliff Blaine, 1969

My sister Scarlett is going to build me a rocket to Jupiter. When she reads peter and Wendy, it makes me think sometimes about flying to Jupiter and being in my rocket ship. peter pan didn't want to grow up, but I think I do because then I can

go to space for real, which is something I can't do
as a kid. Scarlett doesn't want to grow up. I think
because she seems sad sometimes when she talks
about grown-ups. But I think that she will make a
great grown-up some day because she is the best
sister already in the world.

I finished the note, then looked over it again. My eyes devoured every word. I wanted it in my memory forever.

Cliff had faith in me. He believed that I would make it through this world okay and turn out just fine. The knowledge of that fact made me want to believe it too.

I folded up the paper and stuck it back in the book, closing it with a thud. *It may be too late now, but I'm going to build him that rocket.*

● ● ●

Near Christmas, we went to visit Cliff, and the nurses told us that he was allowed to come home with us on Christmas Eve and spend the night, as long as we had him back the next afternoon. So Dad arranged to pick him up in Old Clunker, and we'd let him have his old bedroom back. The only condition was that a nurse had to come along, just to make sure he had someone familiar there. She would sleep on a cot by Cliff's bed in case he needed anything during the night.

I didn't care if a whole team of nurses had to come—Christmas was less than two weeks away, and we finally had something to look forward to. Juli may have left for good, but we'd have the rest of our family together for a solid twenty-four hours. Suddenly, I was glad we decided to decorate a tree.

I had brought Cliff the copy of *Peter and Wendy* in case he decided he wanted to read any more of it. Stacey had asked everyone else to step out in the hallway so they could arrange Cliff's visit home, and since Albert was gone, I found myself alone with Cliff for the first time since his accident. Just the two us. Well, a nurse was sitting in the corner to keep an eye on him. But the nurses were so common there that I could ignore her completely.

I stood at the edge of the bed with the book clasped in my hands. Cliff was propped up on some pillows and still dressed in his pajamas. It was a pair he'd gotten at the home. All minty green with white stripes. He looked at the book in my hands curiously but didn't say anything.

I followed his gaze and held up the book. "This is your favorite book. *Peter and Wendy*. We never finished it. Even once you were gone, we didn't read any of it. Not without you."

He grabbed a candy cane off the bedside table, unwrapped it, and stuck it in his mouth. But he stared at me in silence, as if willing for me to go on.

God, how do I handle this? He's looking at me. My skin tingled. *Oh, God, he actually sees me.*

I licked my lips and opened the book. "We were on the last chapter." I cleared my throat. "Chapter Seventeen. When Wendy grew up …"

He didn't say a word as I read the last chapter. He just watched me. I could feel the nurse in the corner watching me too, taking her eyes off her needlework to look back and forth between us.

The sunlight from the barred window shone onto the pages. My hands were shaking, both from the weight of the book and the thought of Cliff listening to me.

"Of course in the end Wendy let them fly away together. Our last glimpse of her shows her at the window, watching them receding into the sky until they were small as stars."

I glanced at Cliff. His eyes were closed, and he was still sucking on his candy cane, but it seemed like he was paying attention. I don't know if he could comprehend the story or not, but he could tell that I was speaking and he was listening to me.

"As you look at Wendy, you may see her hair becoming white, and her figure little again, for all this happened long ago. Jane is now a common grown-up, with a daughter called Margaret; and every spring cleaning time, except when he forgets, Peter comes for Margaret and takes her to the Neverland, where she tells him stories about himself, to which he listens eagerly. When Margaret grows up, she will have a daughter, who is to be Peter's mother in turn; and thus it will go on, so long as children are gay and innocent and heartless."

I closed the book with a thud. "The End."

Cliff's breathing grew heavier and the leftover stub of candy cane was now clutched in his hand. *I guess he fell asleep again.*

I took a deep breath and let it out, then glanced at the nurse. She looked at me and shrugged before turning back to her needlework.

But he did hear me! He was listening.

"Cliff," I said, my voice soft. I leaned forward until I was touching the gray flannel blanket, clutching it in my fingers. "You may have forgotten, but I'll always remember what I promised you. When you come home on Christmas Eve, there's going to be a big surprise waiting for you."

He muttered something in his sleep. I pressed my lips together. "I promise."

●　●　●

The air was bitterly cold, even for Georgia. I pulled my coat closer across my chest and rubbed my hands together to keep them warm. *Now where did Frank keep those plans?*

I pushed open the door to the bomb shelter and flicked the light switch. The eyes of half a dozen animals blinked up at me, warm and content in their makeshift beds. I grinned. Mildred the chicken was still living and perched on a bed of hay. I wondered if Frank's mother was the one feeding them all. By the looks of it, someone had been in here not too long ago and refilled the food buckets.

Papers were stacked on a small desk on the other side of the shelter. I hopped over a couple turtles and flipped through the pages. *Aha. Frank's plans for Cliff's rocket.*

The door suddenly slammed behind me. I whipped around half-expecting to find Mrs. Leggett standing behind me, very confused as to why I was in her bomb shelter.

Instead my eyes rested on Frank. My mouth dropped open. "Wh— What ..."

An amused smirk played on his lips. He lowered the heavy piece of wood in his hands and stepped back.

I tried to reel my mouth back up, doing my best not to gape at him. "What are you doing here?" Frank had been away at Boston University for the last five months, living out his dream and studying to be a vet. I wasn't sure if I'd ever see him again. I certainly didn't think I'd see him again right now, right here.

He folded his hands behind his back and smirked slightly. "I could ask you the same question, seeing as this is my backyard and no one seems to know you are here."

Guilt pinched at my cheeks. "I'm so sorry," I stammered, stepping back and bumping into the desk. "I just ... I thought that I could ..."

"Scarlet." His face softened into a smile. "You know you're always welcome here."

I gulped. "Thanks." Holding up the paper, I managed an explanation. "I'm building a rocket for Cliff. He's coming home on Christmas Eve, and I want it ready for him. So, I ... I needed the plans."

"Cliff?" A darkness covered Frank's face. I wanted to know what he was thinking. Did he miss Cliff, like I did? Did he wake up every morning expecting to see him, then feel that thud in his chest when he remembered that Cliff wasn't the same anymore? That he was gone?

Frank cleared his throat, like it had suddenly become hard for him to swallow. I looked up just in time to see him glance away quickly. Tears glistened in the corners of his eyes.

The silence hung over us and reminded me of everything we'd lost. That easy friendship between the three of us. That peaceful feeling of knowing everything was fine.

My chest ached. I felt so alone. Even here, with the one other person who might have understood me like Cliff did, I still felt unspeakable pain. My throat felt tight, making it difficult to speak.

"I just ... I should go," I muttered, intending to brush past Frank and run far away.

But instead Frank grabbed me as I walked by and enveloped me in a crushing hug. My face pressed against his shoulder, buried in his jacket. I could tell by his shaking arms that he was crying, and I was crying too. We stood there for what seemed like a century, just hugging and crying and thinking about the summer we'd all shared.

I pulled back and wiped my eyes, and discovred Frank's face was as red and swollen as mine. He rubbed at his cheeks and managed a wobbly smile. Reaching up one finger, he brushed away a tear from the corner of my eye and left his hand there for a moment. "Hey," he said softly, his face only inches away. He smiled at me like he hadn't seen me in years, like the sight of my face was the most wonderful Christmas present he could ever have received. I smiled back and even laughed, which only managed to shake my wet tears down to my coat.

I brushed them away and held up the rocket plans. "So can I have these?"

Frank shook his head. "No." He grew solemn, staring at me.

I blinked. *Is he kidding?* His face remained stony. I felt irritation and a touch of anger beginning to rise. I clutched at the paper. "What? But, Frank …"

He finally cracked a grin. "But you can share them. With me. Because we are going to build that rocket together. I already brought some wood back from Massachusetts, and I intend to see this rocket through to completion, whether you plan on helping or not."

I exhaled, my heartbeat slowing. "Oh. Okay." I folded the paper as gently as possible and placed it in my pocket. "I'm glad. Cliff would have wanted us to do it together."

Frank nodded. "I only have two more weeks off for Christmas break. Then I'm back to school the first week of January."

The buoyant feeling from a moment ago disappeared, and I was glad he couldn't tell. I was afraid to have him know about how much I'd missed him and how completely wonderful it felt to be standing here with him again. "Well then, we'll have to get to work."

● ● ●

"Hot cocoa?" Mrs. Leggett called from the large bay window, waving at us.

I glanced at Frank. "I'm pretty cold. How about you?"

He shrugged. "Some cocoa might be nice."

We pulled off our tool belts and laid them out on the work bench, stepping back to admire our progress. The sides of the rocket were coming together nicely. A few more nails and we would have a pretty fine five-foot rocket. The perfect size for a shortish ten-year-old with a wild imagination.

Mrs. Leggett handed large hot pink mugs of steaming cocoa, with the words *La Vida Loca* painted across the front. "Aren't they just *darling*? I got them from my cha-cha instructor," she explained.

"He always was wildly crazy about me. He begged me to run away and marry him when I was very young, but of course I was too in love with my Luke to even consider it. Although we did have a few great dances together." She flipped her hair over her shoulder and smiled, looking very pleased with herself.

"Yes, Mother," Frank responded, smiling at me over his cocoa. I giggled as his mother rambled on about the technical difficulties of the *darling* cha-cha.

After ten minutes of patiently listening, Frank excused us and led me back outside. "Sorry about that," he said, giving me a sheepish look. "She tends to really go on sometimes."

I grinned and shook my head. "No, I like her. I can tell she really loves you and your dad."

Frank looked up and nodded. "Yeah." A strange light flickered in his eyes. "I know she does."

I couldn't resist adding, "And the cha-cha."

A surprised laugh escaped from Frank and rumbled inside of me. It made me chuckle too, which forced him to laugh even more. We snorted and giggled until our sides hurt, and Frank begged me to stop.

"I hate it when you do that. Because when you laugh, it makes me laugh too," he complained.

I calmed the chuckles still stuck in my throat and concentrated on hammering. "Hey, Frank?"

"Yeah?" He didn't look up. Maybe he was was afraid he'd start laughing again.

"What does the voice in your head sound like?"

"What?"

"I know it sounds silly. But it's just something that Cliff asked you once. You never really answered him, and I never really thought about it."

Frank ran a hand through his hair and looked away. "Do you ever see him anymore? Cliff, I mean."

"Yeah. We drive into the city and visit him every Saturday."

"What's it like?"

"Hard." I straightened and lowered my hands to my side. "He doesn't remember me. Or anything we ever did together." I motioned to the rocket. "He doesn't even remember this."

Frank grimaced, like someone had punched him in the stomach. "I had heard that he wasn't the same, but I had no idea."

I shrugged. "I don't even know why I'm doing this except for the fact that I still remember. And that I'm going to keep my promise to Cliff no matter what. I've realized that I can't keep blaming God for tearing my family apart, or feel guilty for everything I could have done differently. I just have to take each day as it is and try to do the right thing."

"Wow."

I looked down and started hammering again, my face reddening. I'd never meant to get that personal with Frank. "So, um, you didn't answer my question."

"Oh, yeah." Frank stepped back and cocked his head, as if thinking intently. He glanced up with a smirk. "The voice in my head sounds dashingly handsome and mysterious." One of his many cats pranced up and rubbed its head against Frank's leg. He leaned down and scratched between the cat's ears, sending me a wink.

I nudged him. "Seriously." The sound of metal hitting nail resounded in my ears, making them ring. I took another break and rolled the hammer around in my hands. I watched him and noticed how the muscles in his forehead tensed when he thought really hard.

"Well, um ..." Frank took a breath and let it out. "I guess the voice in my head is serious sometimes, maybe most of the time. But sometimes it sounds a little lighthearted. Like it's trying very hard to be good and studious and get things done, but every now and then it just can't resist a little amusement." His face broke in a smile. "Especially when it hears the laugh of a certain freckled girl."

I pressed my lips together. "Yes, I think that perfectly describes what your voice should sound like."

"And let me guess yours." Frank took a step forward, his eyes looking deeply into mine. I shivered at the intense yet kind look reflected in his gaze. "Your voice is sweeter than peach pie and stronger than steel nails and softer than summer clouds."

I took in a sharp breath, unable to tear my eyes away. "Um, yeah, I guess."

He reached out to gently cup my elbow in his palm. At his touch, I jumped. I spun back around to the rocket, accidentally whipping his face with my hair. "Oh, sorry! Um, I …"

He winced and shook his head. "It's okay."

"Yeah, well, um …" I gulped. Things were escalating into a very awkward and still painful territory that I wasn't sure how to navigate. "We should probably get this finished." My voice sounded shaky and tense to me. *Drat.* I squeezed my eyes shut. I gritted my teeth and hammered in another nail. *Stupid, stupid Scarlett.*

● ● ●

My brush swept across the wood in smooth, even strokes. Electric-green paint, exactly the color of Cliff's crayon drawing.

The sun felt a bit warmer, providing a little relief in the cold winter. I glanced up and saw Mrs. Leggett watching me from the window. I smiled and waved. She nodded before the curtain fell back into place.

Frank wasn't home. He'd gone to the grocery store to pick up a few things for Christmas supper, his mother had told me. But I couldn't wait for him to paint the rocket. It needed to get done by that night. Christmas Eve.

A chilly breeze tickled my neck and pulled at my loose waves.

With a paint-splattered hand, I reached back and pushed at my hair, managing to smear green paint on my cheek. Drat. I attempted to wipe it away, likely only smudging it further.

I give up. I dropped the brush back into the bucket of paint. Then I grabbed a fresh brush to dip in red for the finishing touch. *To Jupiter*, written with a Cliff-like scrawl.

I put down the paint brush and stood back, pulling off my smock. I placed my hands on my ruined blue jeans and sighed. It was perfect. Absolutely perfect.

"Wonderful," someone whispered.

I turned around to see Frank beaming from ear to ear.

"I thought you were at the grocery store."

"I was." He held up two large paper bags, one in each arm. "And I returned only to find you in my backyard. And I suppose my mother is …" He glanced at the house and nodded grimly. His mother was standing at the window watching us. "Just as I suspected. Here, let me drop off these groceries, and then I'll take you on a walk." Without waiting for my response, he ran back to the house and returned a few short minutes later. He immediately looped his arm through mine and began strolling toward the orchards. "Come, let us discuss the success of Cliff's rocket."

"Um, okay." I tried not to focus on how close he was standing to me and how blurry my thoughts were.

We rambled through the orchards of bare peach trees without talking much at all. Instead, we stopped before each tree and stared at the naked branches, sometimes glancing at each other with a small smile. It felt strange to be walking together again. Almost as if we were adults trying to remember what it was like to be kids. But could that really be possible after only a few short months?

A thousand thoughts ran across my mind as we walked in silence. I thought about Cliff, about the rocket, about our summer of picking peaches, and how great it would be if we put the rocket by the pond.

"I've been doing some thinking," I said slowly, glancing at Frank.

He shot me a teasing grin. "Really?"

"Yes, really." I rolled my eyes. Then I looked away, focusing on the ground below me. "I prayed for God to give me a purpose. Something to do that would please him and take my mind off all the pain."

"And has he?" Frank's voice was quiet.

I wrapped my arms across my chest and looked up at the sky. "Yeah. I think so." I glanced at Frank. He was watching me, a thoughtful smile on his face. "I want to travel," I told him. "I want to see all the places Cliff only dreamed about. I want to tell people about his hopes and dreams and find out about other people too." A new thought occurred to me. "I want to fill others with the same hope that God has given me every time I think of Cliff's hopes and dreams. Even if he doesn't remember them now, that doesn't mean they can't inspire a whole new group of people."

Frank nodded. We walked in silence for a while, thinking about the future.

"You know." Frank cleared his throat and tightened his grip on my arm. I glanced at him, surprised to see his face slowly turning a bright shade of red. He looked at me and looked away. "I was thinking too. You know, while I was away at college."

I grinned, deciding to tease him back. "You were thinking? At college? *Astounding.*"

He didn't smile back, only puckered his brow more. "I did a lot of thinking about … Um, well, you know … I took a good look at my heart, and I know now that I've loved—"

Oh, no. I suddenly felt like my body weighed four hundred pounds. *There is no way I can live through this again. No way I can handle him rejecting me for Juli again while I stand here like a stupid, silent ragdoll.* I bit my lips as words gushed out of me too fast to comprehend. "You know what? I just really ..." I could feel my breath speed up as I broke away from him. "I have to go. I'll see you tonight."

I shouted good-bye over my shoulder and bolted, ignoring the judging looks I was sure the empty trees were giving me. *Coward.* I shivered, pulling my jacket over my cheeks. *You just can't handle the shame. Can't handle feeling second best.*

My stomach churned. I needed to be brave. Fearless. *Maybe I should go back and ...*

I glanced over my shoulder. Frank was still standing in the same spot, hands in his pockets, his shoulders slumped. His face was too far away to read. I wondered if he even saw me looking.

Squaring my shoulders, I focused on the road in front of me and quickened my pace back home.

Chapter 18

The smell of peppermint filled the house, drifting from the kitchen into the living room where we stood looking at the tree. All the lights were on, filling the room with dazzling brilliance. A little angel twinkled at us from her perch on top of the tree.

Mama sighed and buttoned up her coat. It was pretty cold outside for Georgia. "Are you ready to go?"

I nodded. Pulling on my jacket, I gave my hair a final pat. My unruly waves were somewhat tamed for the moment, pulled back into a loose twist. I was dressed in my old cranberry red velvet dress, which was a little small but still long enough to cover my knees. *This is almost too much even for the church service. I still don't know why we have to be this dressed up to go get Cliff. It's not like he'll notice.*

Catching myself, I pushed that thought out of my mind and tried again. *It's sweet that we're dressing up. Mama's just trying to make things nice.*

"Okay, I'll go fire up Old Clunker," Dad said, grabbing the keys from the kitchen table. He winked and disappeared out the side door.

I glanced back at Mama. She was staring at the tree with haunted eyes. Her arms were wrapped around her chest. Her eyes flickered toward me. "I'm okay," she said, reading the worry on my face. She let out a deep breath. "I'll be in the truck. You go get Grandpop Barley."

I trudged up the steps, taking two at a time. Grandpop Barley's door was closed. When I pushed it open I found him sitting on the edge of the bed in his best Sunday jacket. My eyebrows flew up. "Grandpop Barley! You … you look very nice. All ready for church and the trip to get Cliff."

He stared at me blankly, his eyes empty of emotion. I watched him for a moment, waiting. *Well, what did you expect? Him to answer back?* I rolled my eyes. "Okay, come on. We need to get to the truck. Mama and Dad are waiting, and you know that look Mama gets when we head into the sanctuary after the bell tolls." I looped my arm through his and led him out the door.

I heard a car coming down the driveway. I paused in the doorway, frowning. *Who would be coming here on Christmas Eve?*

I rushed Grandpop Barley down the stairs and out the door. My mouth dropped open at the sight in front of me.

Stepping out of her beat-up car, Juli stared at us from behind shaggy bangs. She slammed the door and yawned. "Wow, I'm really beat." Then she passed out in a dead faint in the driveway.

● ● ●

Few things in my life have felt stranger than standing in my doorway that afternoon and watching my sister sleeping in my bedroom. Beams of light from the hallway behind me cast shadows on her pale face.

"Who is going to go get Cliff if Juli's here?" Mama whispered. "We shouldn't leave her alone."

Amen to that. Judging by the way Juli looked, I doubted she could be left alone for five minutes, much less several hours. Awake or not.

"She needs her sleep," Dad said firmly, shutting the door to my room. We stood in the hallway with our hands in our coat pockets. "Scarlett, do you mind staying here to make sure she is okay until we get back? If she wakes up, make sure she eats something." His voice grew rough. "She doesn't look like she's eaten a thing since she left."

I pressed my lips together and nodded. *Babysitting Juli. Sounds like fun.* My face flushed, even though I was sure no one had heard me think that. My sister just came back from months away in who knows where, and she was safe and sleeping and warm. I really had no cause to be bitter or cynical.

Mama put her coat back on and glanced at the door again. "Are you sure we should both go? What if she wants us?"

Dad sighed. "She needs to sleep. She'll be fine for a couple hours, and Scarlett's a good caretaker." He rested an arm around Mama's shoulder, pressing his lips to her temple. "Come on. We're already going to be late to church."

They each gave me a quick hug before disappearing with Grandpop Barley. I could hear Old Clunker rev up and drive away, lost in a cloud of dust.

I trudged downstairs to the kitchen and made myself a bologna sandwich. Settling on the sofa, I flipped through old cookbooks in the vain hope of finding something exciting and unsentimental to cook for Christmas supper. We didn't need a warm, mushy family meal to remind us of how everything was more bland and awkward this year. We needed spicy tacos or fried fish. Something that could become our new Christmas meal.

Every now and then, my eyes flickered to the ceiling, and I imagined Juli curled up under my sheets. Her face had seemed so thin and gaunt, her skin pale to the point of being translucent. I shivered. What horrible things had she been doing?

I squeezed my eyes shut. *God, I don't know what's wrong with*

Juli, but please fix her inside. Sew up all those fraying threads and gaping holes and make her whole again.

When she's ready, I'm going to talk to her about the same things Mrs. Greene told me. Just that thought made me feel ten times better. Maybe she'd be able to experience the same peace that I did.

The sound of tires on the gravel startled me to attention. My skin bristled. *It's too early for them to be home.* A shiver ran down my spine. With Juli upstairs and the rest of the family on their way to get Cliff, who else would be coming here?

Heavy footsteps pounded on the front steps. A loud knock followed on the door.

I walked toward the front door, unlatched the lock, and swung it open. *Frank.*

He was dressed in a button-down shirt and necktie, his hair slicked back like Sunday mornings when we were kids. Only a few stray hairs had escaped and flopped on his forehead, like he'd been in a rush to get here.

My mouth seemed caught between a smile and a frown. I shook my head. "What are you doing here?"

He shrugged. "I was a little worried when you didn't show up for the Christmas Eve service. I thought we had the whole thing figured out. You know, with the unveiling of the rocket and everything? And then when your parents came in late without you …" He took a deep breath and puffed it out. "I knew I couldn't bolt across the church and ask where you were, so I snuck out the back instead."

"Oh." My mouth felt dry. "Well, you didn't have to panic on my account."

He blinked. "I just … I wanted to make sure you were okay."

His words sunk into my head slowly. He just wanted to check on me. That look on his face—those stray hairs falling on his forehead—that was all because he was worried about me.

He didn't know about Juli being back, though. How much faster would he have ran if he'd known she was sleeping upstairs?

I forced a smile. "I'm fine." *Say it. Just say it.* "Juli's home." The words felt like ice on my tongue.

Frank's eyes widened. "Really?" He glanced over my shoulder and into the house. "Wow. I mean, that's unexpected."

"I know." I searched his face, every crease and crinkle of it. Searching for signs that he'd missed her. That he was desperate to see her again.

Instead, he looked back at me with a small smile. "Is she asleep? Could you be excused for a few minutes?"

This time, I was the one blinking like a deer caught in the headlights. "I'd have to go check on her. I don't want to leave her alone."

He nodded, and I ran upstairs and pushed open the bedroom door. Juli was lying in bed with her eyes open, staring at the ceiling. "Oh, hey," she said when she saw me.

I swallowed hard. "Hi. I was just ... I wanted to make sure you're okay and I ..."

"Whose car is that?"

So she knew someone was here. Well, no use prolonging the inevitable. "Frank's."

"Did he come to see you?"

"Yeah." *I think so.* "But I'm just going to send him home. I don't want to leave you here and—"

"Scarlett." Juli's voice was soft, and she smiled slightly. "I just came home. I'm not going to leave again just yet, okay? I'll still be here when you get back."

I paused. "Are you sure?"

"Positive."

I trusted her. For the first time in who knows how many months, I trusted Juli's words. "Okay. I'll be back soon." I shut the door and ran back downstairs.

Frank was still standing in the hallway, hands in his pockets. "So can you come?"

"I guess. Let me grab my coat."

I picked at the hem of my itchy velvet dress as I followed Frank outside. The winter air was cold and dry, and dark clouds covered the moon. "I think it's supposed to snow," Frank said, motioning to the sky. "In Georgia. It's a record or something."

"Huh." I was only half listening, concentrating on wrapping my arms around myself to keep warm.

We walked down the driveway until the house was only barely visible. I reminded Frank that I should stay close for Juli's sake.

He nodded. "I'm glad she came home. She's better off here."

I managed an *uh-hmm*. It hurt to talk about Juli with him. Each word was a painful reminder of what I would never have with Frank. Not that I cared. *Because I don't care about Frank in that way anymore. Right?*

I glanced at him sideways. "If I were you, I wouldn't come on to Juli too strongly at first. Give her time to recover. And then try to win her over slowly. Make her laugh." I puffed out my cheeks. "And be good to her."

Frank stopped in his tracks, pivoting on his heels until he stood a few inches away from me. He raised a brow. "Am I to understand that you want me to woo Juli?"

I felt pinned under his gaze. I was sure my cheeks were turning red. "Um, I thought you wanted to."

Shaking his head slowly, Frank took another step toward me. "I … I am such a complete and utter fool. Stupid. Idiotic. Thick-headed. Pea-brained." His voice heated with anger.

My lip quivered. I started to open my mouth, but he held up a hand to stop me.

He pushed a hand through his hair, messing up whatever the hair gel was supposed to keep neat. There were no stray pieces anymore because it was pretty much all falling on his forehead and over his ears. "It's always been me and you, Scarlett," he whispered, his eyes intense in the shaded moonlight. He reached up and touched my cheek. "I was so stupid not to see it before. Not to see that you are everything I …" He trailed off, turning red. He dropped his hand and stuck it in his pocket. "Drat," he muttered. Avoiding my eyes, he sighed and stared at the ground. "I'm really bad at making speeches. It's not going to sound like it should."

I sucked in air but felt no oxygen. Suddenly, the cold night felt burning hot. My heart felt caught in between soaring and falling. Waiting for a single word from Frank to tell me which direction to go.

He glanced up. "Okay, let me try again." A smile pulled at his mouth as he grabbed my hand. This time, he looked right at me, unashamed. "Scarlett, I like you. I like you more than cats, more than dogs, more than peach pie and bicycles." He laughed. "I like you more than any other person in Georgia. I think I love you."

My throat caught, resulting in an unattractive strangled sound. I winced and held back a grimace. *Great. I've waited months for this guy to really like me, and now I'm going to scare him away with my repressed gagging.*

Frank just chuckled. "I love how offbeat and thoughtful you are. How you make me see things I've never seen before and care about things I didn't even know about. I loved watching you with Cliff and the way you care about him even though others don't understand him. The way you radiate light even on a cloudy day." His finger reached up and looped around a strand of my hair, pulling it gently. "I love every freckle on your nose and the sky in your eyes and the way your hair goes in every direction." He paused. "I think your hair is really pretty, by the way, even though I know you hate it."

I was vaguely conscious of the fact that I was rocking back and forth on my toes. My insides were singing, bubbling with joy and laughter.

"Scarlett, I …" Frank's voice grew serious, as his face softened. "You just turned seventeen. I'm only eighteen. But I …" He cleared his throat. "I'm too young to be married. I still have three more years of college and then I have to find a job, but after that …"

I bit my lip as he trailed off into silence, staring at me. The quiet burned at me. I ached to know. "After that what?" I finally asked.

His hands dropped from my hair and grabbed mine, lacing our fingers together. "I want you to wait for me," he whispered. "And then I want to be with my best friend forever. I'll build us a house. We'll have a green roof and lots of windows and the largest kitchen in Georgia."

I rolled my eyes. "If your house-building skills are anything like your rocket ones, then you're going to need my help." Which was a total lie. Because Frank was probably the best carpenter I'd ever laid eyes on. But I wanted to think that he'd want my help some day. That he'd need me by his side.

Frank jabbed at me with his elbow. "Hey, I'm pretty good with tools!"

I snorted, causing him to jab me more. "Stop it." I wiggled away, turning my back to him. Something wet dropped on my nose. My eyes widened. "It's snowing!"

Sure enough, fluffy white snowflakes fell from the sky, enveloping us in a frosty wonderland. They reflected off the porch lights as they swirled around in the air. I closed my eyes and spun around, my arms outstretched. I couldn't remember the last time I saw snow in Georgia, or the last time I saw snow anywhere.

"Scarlett." Frank's voice dropped, causing me to stop and slowly turn back around.

He watched me with the most contented smile. Like he wasn't looking for Juli or some sophisticated woman or beauty queen, but he was happy just to see *me*. Scarlett.

"What do you say?" he whispered.

A light layer of snow clung to my hair, wetting my cheeks. I stepped closer until our foreheads nearly touched. "I love you," I whispered. "And I'd wait forever for you."

He smiled, which made me smile, and we stood there like two grinning fools until headlights shone in front of us, and my parents were home. They piled out of the car and seemed surprised to see Frank, but no one asked any questions. Instead, they took care to lead Cliff into the house, and then headed upstairs to make sure Juli was okay.

Once everyone was in the house, I fixed bologna sandwiches and served them while we waited for my parents to come down so we could go see the finished rocket. Cliff sat at the counter next to his nurse and ate his sandwich quietly, glancing at me and Frank but not saying anything. He looked around the house as if everything was new, taking in the sight of the Christmas tree and the dining room table and the big window in the kitchen.

Frank looked at me and sighed, and I could tell from the look in his eyes that he was just as sad as I was. But we managed to smile and tried to say a few things to Cliff, even if he wasn't talking back.

"I never told you how much I like your kitchen," Frank said, licking a drop of mustard off his finger. He looked around. "It defines you. As an excellent cook, I mean."

"Thanks." My legs dangled off the edge of the barstool. "I pretty much get to keep it in whatever order I want since I'm the only one who cooks in it anyway." I drummed my fingers on the countertop. "I run a pretty tight ship, though."

Frank nodded and finished his sandwich. He brushed the crumbs off his dress pants and placed his plate in the sink just as my parents walked in.

"Okay," Dad said, pulling on his coat. "Juli is awake and has promised to stay here tonight. She seems okay, although she's as hungry as two teenage boys. And then some." He shook his head. "Okay, Cliff, are you ready to go for another ride in the truck?"

Mama opened the screen door for us and ushered us outside and into Old Clunker. Since there wasn't enough room for us all inside, Frank and I climbed into the bed of the truck. Snow danced around in the headlights as we rolled down the dirt road toward Frank's farm.

"What if he doesn't respond? What if he gets angry and throws a fit? What if—?"

In the darkness, I felt Frank's hand slip into my own, his fingers laced tightly through mine.

"It's going to be okay. No matter what, it'll be okay."

"Thanks," I whispered, giving his palm a tight squeeze.

No lights were on at Frank's house. His parents must have already tucked in for the night, unconcerned about their son's sudden disappearance at the Christmas Eve service.

Frank led us to the backyard and pulled a flashlight out of his pocket. The beam of light fell on a large heap covered by a white sheet. "There it is," he said, motioning for me to pass ahead of him. "Scarlett, would you like to do the honors?"

I nodded and moved toward the rocket. My heart was beating wildly. Cliff stood by my parents, shivering in his lightweight jacket. He stared at the covered rocket curiously, all the while gripping his nurse's hand. Every now and then, he'd mutter something under his breath or twitch.

It's now or never.

Swiftly, I reached out and pulled off the sheet. It fluttered in the wind, caught for a brief moment in the wild dance of the snowflakes, before settling on the already frosty ground.

In the moonlight, the rocket almost shined a translucent green. Frank waved the flashlight over the words *To Jupiter* and the window, where we had carefully painted in all of our faces dressed in astronaut garb. A drawing of Cliff waved from the commander's seat with a cheeky smile.

I spun around and looked at Cliff. He stared at it blankly, his eyes not blinking. Then he turned and tugged on his nurse's arm, muttering something in gibberish.

Mama gave us a small smile and nodded. "It's very nice, Scarlett."

"Well done," Dad said. He rubbed the toe of his boot on the ground. "Well done."

My throat burned. *That's it? That's all they have to say?*

The nurse cleared her throat and took a step forward. "Cliff says that he's cold and wants to go back. I think he's had enough." She frowned apologetically before taking him by the arm and walking him back toward the truck.

Mama pressed her lips together then glanced at Dad. "Come on, let's go back to the truck. I want to get my boy back home and in his own bed."

He nodded and rested his arm around her shoulder, leading her back to Old Clunker.

I watched them go and blinked back tears. Cliff's shoulders gently swayed as he walked away, one foot in front of the other. That wasn't *my* Cliff. My Cliff would have shouted for joy in Spanish at the sight of his completed rocket. He would have been grabbing *my* hand, not this strange nurse's. This was his dream, and he was just walking away.

"He didn't get it," I whispered. "I don't understand. Why didn't he get it?"

Frank reached out and cupped my elbow in his hand, drawing me toward him. "He doesn't remember the Cliff that we do," he whispered into my hair. "He may be the same person, but he doesn't remember those dreams. You saw him. You *know* Cliff, Scarlett. And you know that behind that battered brain, deep back there, this ..."

He motioned toward the rocket. "*This* is exactly what he would have wanted."

I stood back and rested my head on Frank's shoulder, staring at the rocket in the moonlight. I was okay with Cliff not understanding. He didn't need to understand. I didn't build the rocket because of that.

It was all for his dream, or for the memory of it. Deep down inside, I knew that he saw it. The beauty of that hunk of wood and those sheets of metal. All of the childish hopes and dreams. All of the wishes and imagination. It was real. Here. Now.

Cliff was halfway across the yard by now, on his way to the truck. I could tell that he was saying something to his nurse because he tugged her arm and looked up at her. Then, something happened. A moment that I'll never forget.

His lips still moving, Cliff glanced over his shoulder and took one more look at the rocket. And then, just like that day in the mental facility, he smiled. Really, actually, *smiled*.

And, of course, I smiled too, even though he had turned around by then and was making his way toward Old Clunker.

You know what, Cliff? I thought back on all the conversations and giggles and moments we had shared. *Somewhere along the way, I think I finally grew up. And it wasn't because I suddenly became smart or popular or pretty. It was because of you.*

I leaned against Frank's chest and sighed. Everything felt so much better now. It really was amazing, actually.

"I think you did a pretty fantastic job," Frank said, his chest rumbling under my head.

"I agree."

I turned to see Dad walking back toward me. "It looks great," he said with a smile. I stepped forward, and he slipped his arm around my shoulder. He squeezed me close to him and nodded, smiling at the rocket. Bending down to kiss my forehead, I caught a whiff of his aftershave and felt the way his beard tickled my skin. My eyelids slid shut, forcing myself to remember this moment. These few brief seconds when everything seemed not only okay, but also wonderful. The world was at peace, my family was together again, and Cliff was here with us.

Dad pulled back and patted my shoulder. "Come on, Scarlett. Just about time to go home. I'll give you two a minute, but we need to head back. We may only have one night where we'll all be together like this, and I mean to make the most of it." He gave me one last squeeze before I was alone again with Frank and his flashlight.

I sighed and gave the rocket one last look over. My mind was a flurry. Gratitude and happiness and peacefulness all mixed up.

God ... I squeezed my eyes shut, unsure what to say. *Thank you*, I finally decided. *Thank you for right here and right now. For all the little things you've given me.*

"I'll see you tomorrow," Frank was saying, turning the flashlight away from the rocket. He picked up the sheet and draped it back into place.

I began walking back to the truck. "Are you coming back to our house for your car?"

"Nah." He shook his head, causing snowflakes to fall to the ground. "I'll get it tomorrow. I need a reason to come see you anyway."

"It's Christmas. Isn't that reason enough?"

He nodded. "Merry Christmas, Scarlett."

As I walked back to the car, Mama and Dad were standing by the door hand in hand. They were smiling and looking up at the moon, watching the snowflakes drift across the sky.

I stopped and grinned. *Merry Christmas.*

● ● ●

Every story has to end somewhere. And I don't know how mine is going to end just yet, but you know what? That's okay.

I'd like to think I finally grew up that summer. Finally fell in love, finally found my place in the world. We all get to a point in life where we are standing on the brink, and we have to jump.

Frank did become a veterinarian, and we now have a house over-brimming with rescued animals. We hope to have children who have their father's way with animals. In the meantime, we both volunteer at the children's hospital from time to time, and try to make some of the kids' dreams come true. Like the one girl who wanted to see the ocean—we decorated her room like an undersea paradise, and I can still remember how her eyes lit up when we took her inside.

I only live about an hour from Cliff and not far from the rest of my family. I can see him once a week, and even though he still doesn't say much, sometimes, if I visit often enough, he remembers who I am. And because of that, I realize that we're all going to be just fine.

A few years ago, we went back to Frank's parents' house and moved the rocket we'd built. With a fresh coat of paint, it was ready for its new home on the edge of our yard. I can see it outside of my kitchen window. Every morning, when I do the dishes, I look at that sign and thank God for the hope he's given me.

Life isn't always filled with sunshine and laughter. I've had my share of heartaches, just like everyone else. And I know that God's plan is to give his peace for those who struggle, even if it takes some time for us to see his plans. And I think that would be a pretty great thing to paint on a sign. In Spanish or not.

Enjoy this excerpt from Rachel Coker's debut novel, *Interrupted*.

"A feel-good story for both heart and soul." —Kirkus
"Coker is one to watch." —Publisher's Weekly

A NOVEL

interrupted

life beyond words

Rachel Coker

Chapter 1

A chilly Peace infests the Grass
The Sun respectful lies —
Not any Trance of industry
These shadows scrutinize.

—Emily Dickinson

I stared at the ceiling in silence. Although it was so dark I don't think it could really be called staring at all. More like tilting my chin up in that direction.

My room was cold and quiet, the moon casting eerie shadows through my window over the things that, at thirteen years old, I held dear. My china doll, my stuffed bears, my book collection ...

"Alcyone," a voice whispered.

I gasped and jerked my head toward the door.

Mama stood by my bed, clad in a milky-white nightgown, her long, dark hair falling down her shoulders. She held a finger up to her lips.

"Come on, Allie," she whispered, grabbing my wrist gently. "I want you to see the stars."

My heart still thumping, I followed her down the hallway, my bare feet pattering on the cold wooden floor. The moon shone on the clock by the staircase. 2:52.

I rubbed my eyes groggily. "Where are we——"

Mama halted in the doorway of the kitchen, the moonlight illuminating her from the back.

"Close your eyes."

I did, and let her lead me out the little door until I could feel the damp grass between my toes. I shivered at everything I could feel and sense: the chilly air, the chirping crickets, the dewy earth ...

"Open them," Mama commanded, lowering her hold from my wrist to my hand.

I did, and the first thing I saw was heaven, the way it was meant to look from earth.

Millions of dazzling stars were strung across the sky above us. Twinkling and dancing and *singing*. My heart skipped a beat.

I knelt on the ground beside Mama and stretched back to see as much of the sky as possible. It just seemed to go on and on, covering the fields around us with a sweet and heavy blanket.

I tilted my head and racked my brain for words to describe it. *Eerie ... dreamy ... alluring ... enthralling ... breathtaking.*

"The moon is distant from the sea," Mama murmured, "and yet with amber hands, she leads him, docile as a boy, along appointed sands."

I turned to look at Mama. She was staring at the sky, a strange look on her face. She was so beautiful ... so light and delicate.

I was confused. "Mama," I whispered, "we aren't at the sea." I'd never been to the sea, and I was quite sure she hadn't been in many, many years.

Mama's lips upturned in a little smile. "That was Dickinson." She reached over and stroked my cheek. Her eyes had a far-off mist. "One day you'll understand, Allie. One day you'll be a great writer too."

"Is that what you want of me?" I whispered.

Mama nodded slowly, stroking my cheek. "Yes, my miracle. I want you to write and I want you to be happy."

I longed to ask more questions, but Mama was so peaceful that night I rolled back around and stared at the stars in silence while Mama sang softly in French. I painted in my mind the sweetest dream of a lifetime spent gardening the stars.

Mama had a beautiful voice. It was high and clear. When she sang it sounded like dozens of little tinkling bells. I used to lie awake in bed and listen to her play the piano and sing from the foyer until my eyelids slid down and shut.

For the last six years, it had been the two of us, just like this. I was born when Mama thought she was already an old woman: 1925, the year she turned forty-seven. She always called me her "miracle baby" as a result.

All Mama and I had were each other. Mama said that the world was full of people — and people are full of evil. She told me there was no one and nothing you could trust but where you come from and who you are. We didn't talk to those evil people. We kept to ourselves and spent our time keeping busy.

I heard a meow from across the yard. "Daphne," I whispered, holding out my hands for my little orange kitten. I held her close and whispered in her little feline ears the names of the different constellations. "And that one right there is Taurus—it holds the star Alcyone, just like my name. See, Daphne?" I yawned, smiling. Daphne purred and settled her head on my stomach. I stared at my namesake. "I'm a star, aren't I?"

The moon began to grow hazy and dim as my eyelids started to drop. Mama rubbed my back with one hand and sang to herself as I drifted off to sleep.

Talk It Up!

Want free books?
First looks at the best new fiction?
Awesome exclusive merchandise?

We want to hear from you!

Give us your opinions on titles, covers, and stories.
Join the Z Street Team.

Visit zstreetteam.zondervan.com/joinnow
to sign up today!

Also—Friend us on Facebook!

www.facebook.com/goodteenreads

- Video Trailers
- Connect with your favorite authors
- Sneak peeks at new releases
- Giveaways
- Fun discussions
- And much more!